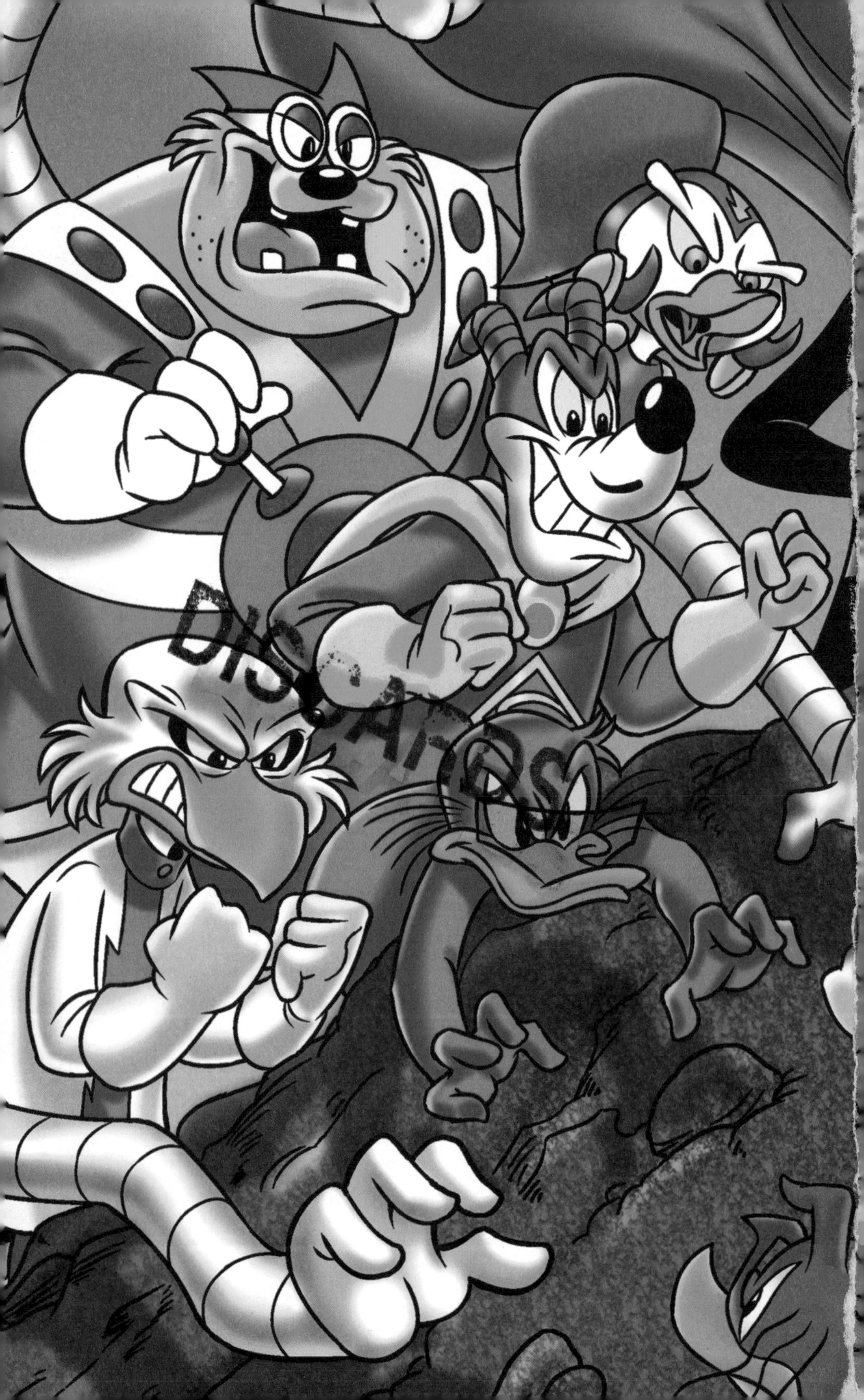

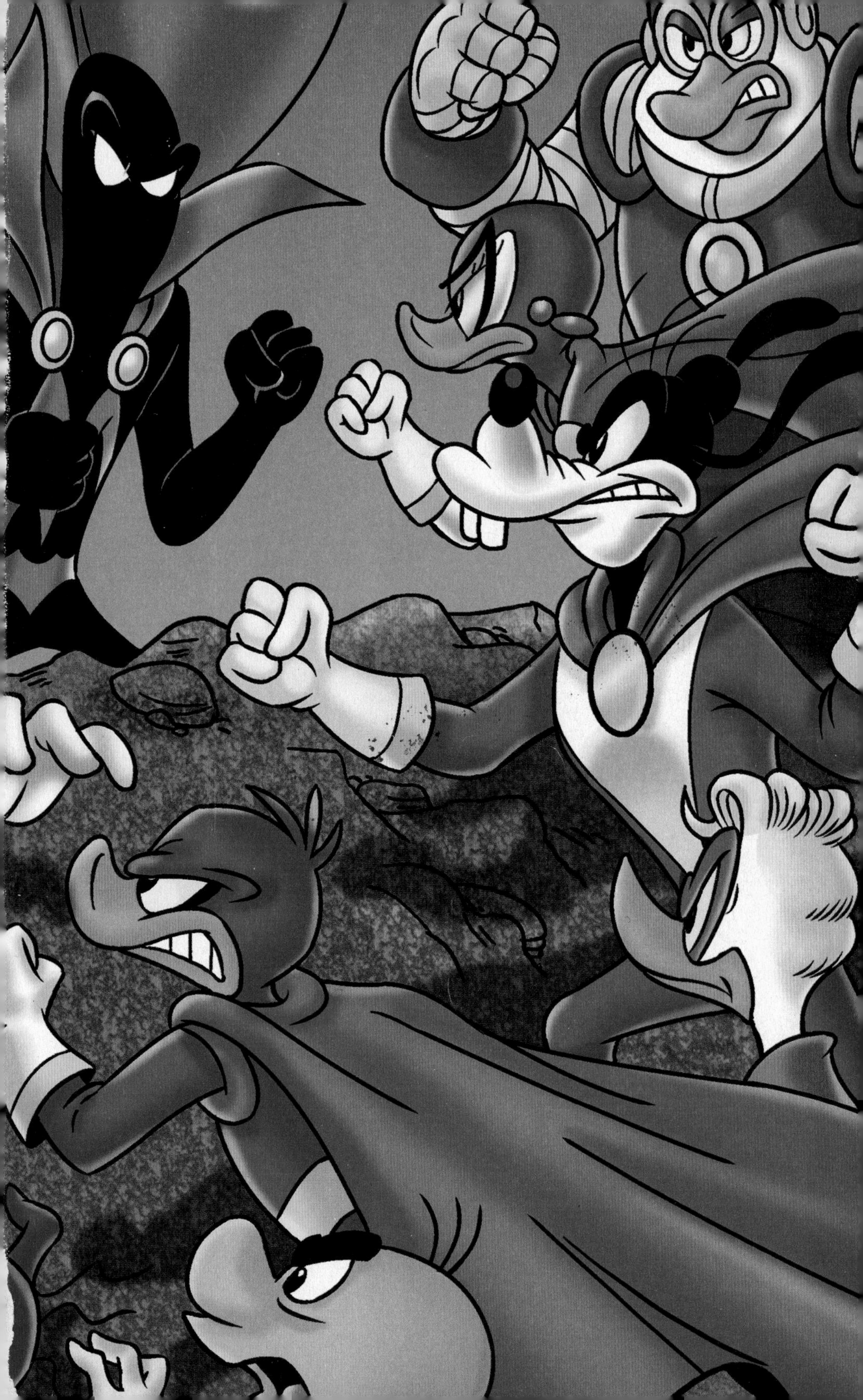

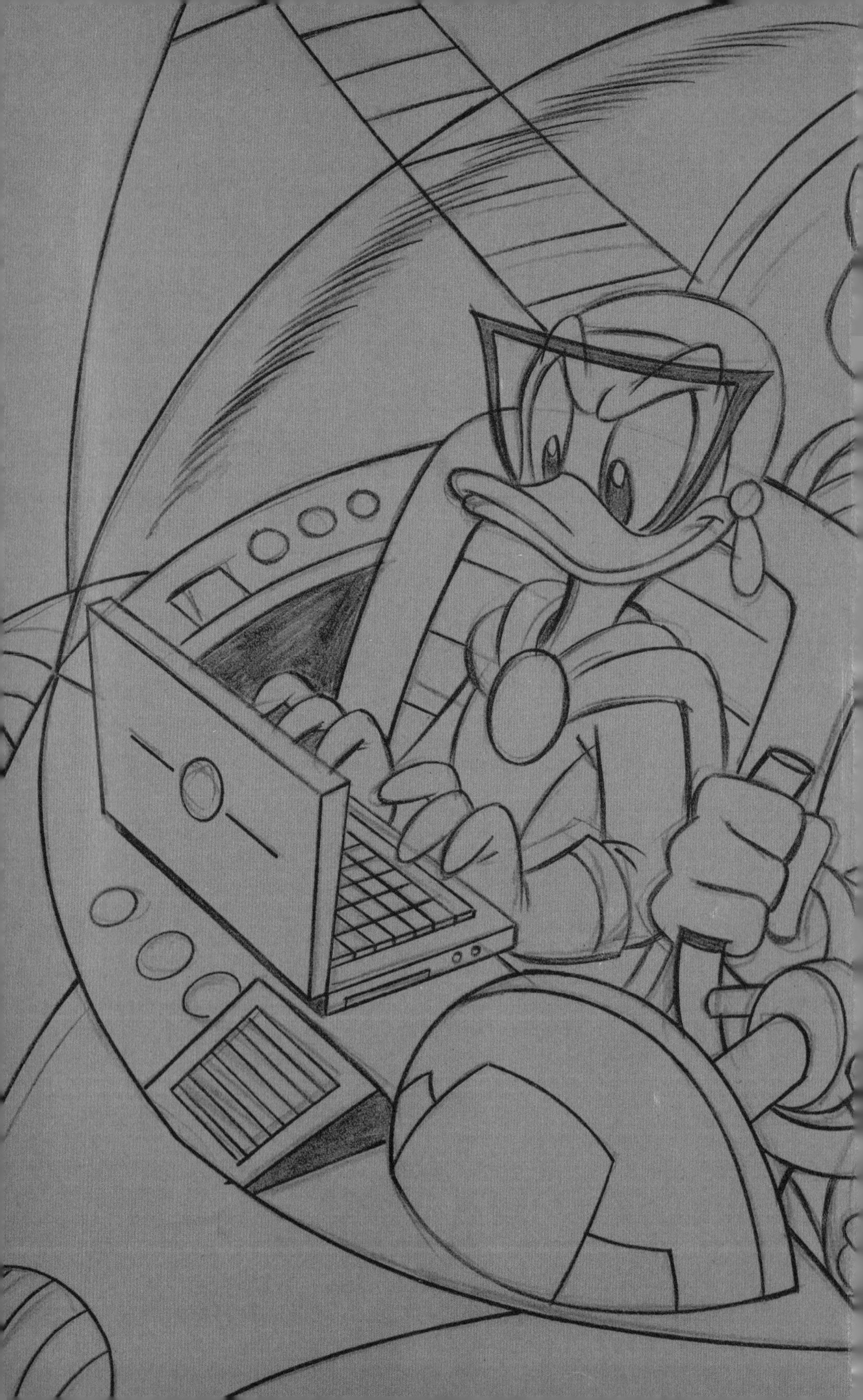

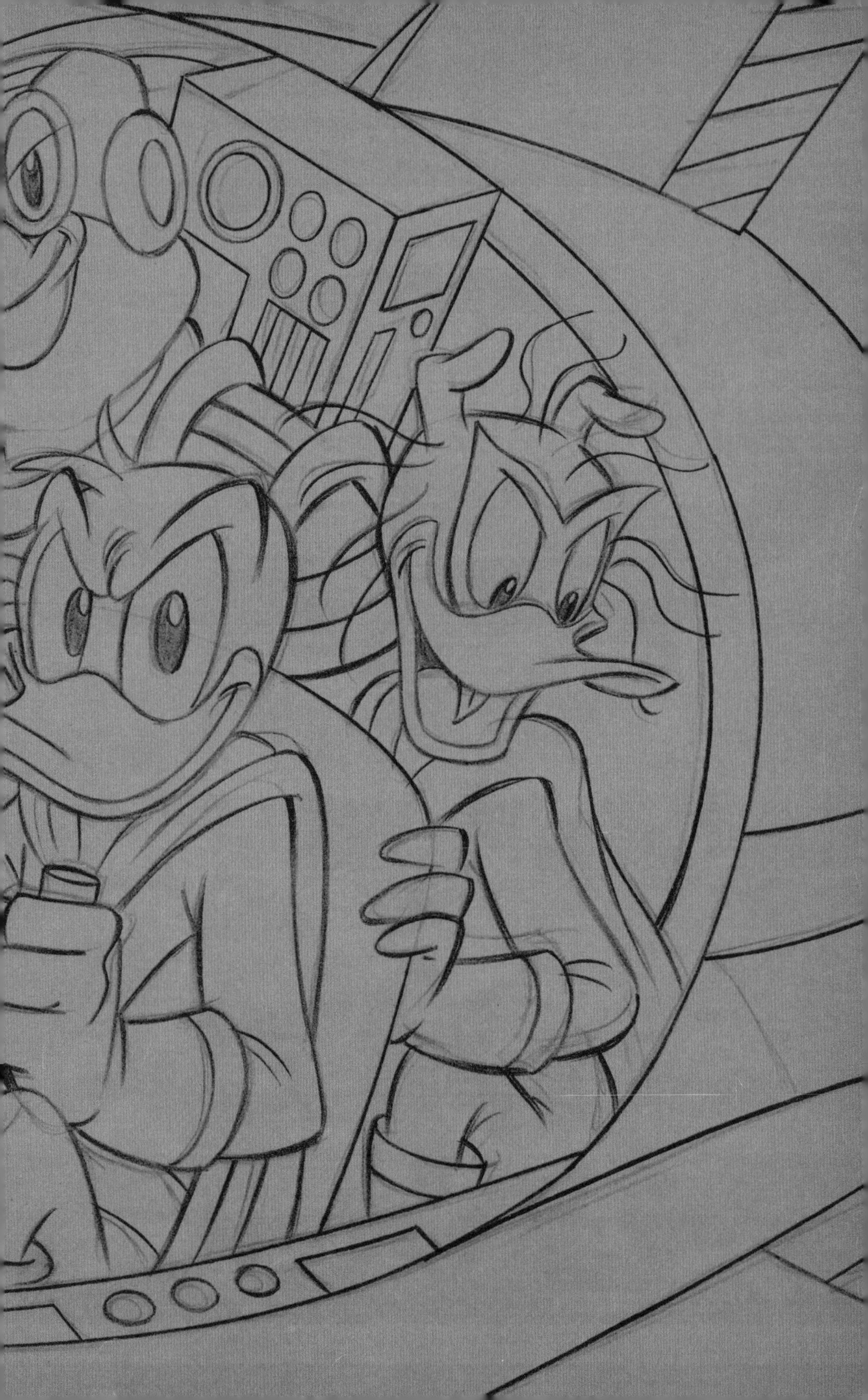

DISNEY'S HERO SQUAD ULTRAHEROES

ROSS RICHIE
chief executive officer

MARK WAID
editor-in-chief

ADAM FORTIER
vice president,
publishing

CHIP MOSHER
marketing director

MATT GAGNON
managing editor

JENNY CHRISTOPHER
sales director

FIRST EDITION: JANUARY 2010

10 9 8 7 6 5 4 3 2 1
PRINTED BY WORLD COLOR PRESS, INC.
ST. ROMUALD, QC, CANADA

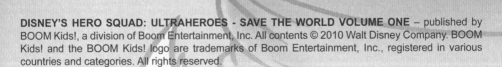

DISNEY'S HERO SQUAD: ULTRAHEROES - SAVE THE WORLD VOLUME ONE – published by BOOM Kids!, a division of Boom Entertainment, Inc. All contents © 2010 Walt Disney Company. BOOM Kids! and the BOOM Kids! logo are trademarks of Boom Entertainment, Inc., registered in various countries and categories. All rights reserved.

Office of publication: 6310 San Vicente Blvd Ste 404, Los Angeles, CA 90048-5457.

A catalog record for this book is available from OCLC and on our website www.boom-kids.com on the Librarians page.

WRITERS:
RICCARDO SECCHI, ALESSANDRO FERRARI
& GIORGIO SALATI

ARTISTS:
STEFANO TURCONI, ANTONELLO DALENA,
ETTORE GULA & EMILIO URBANO

EDITOR:
AARON SPARROW

COVER:
STEFANO TURCONI

HARDCOVER CASE WRAP:
MAGIC EYE STUDIOS

TRANSLATOR:
SAIDA TEMOFONTE

LETTERER:
DERON BENNETT

SPECIAL THANKS:
JESSE POST, LAUREN
KRESSEL & ELENA GARBO

ASSISTANT EDITOR:
CHRISTOPHER BURNS

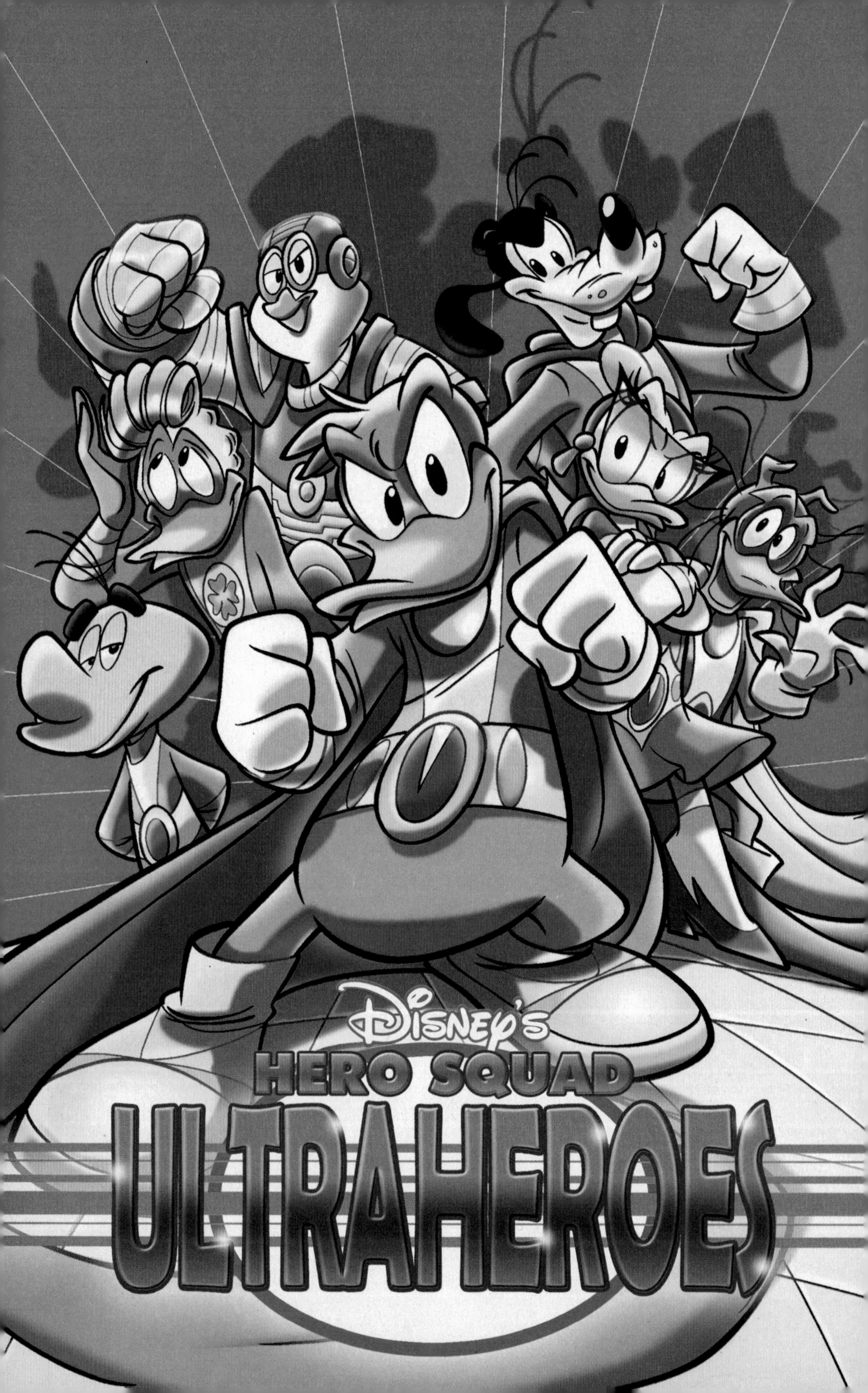
DISNEY'S
HERO SQUAD
ULTRAHEROES

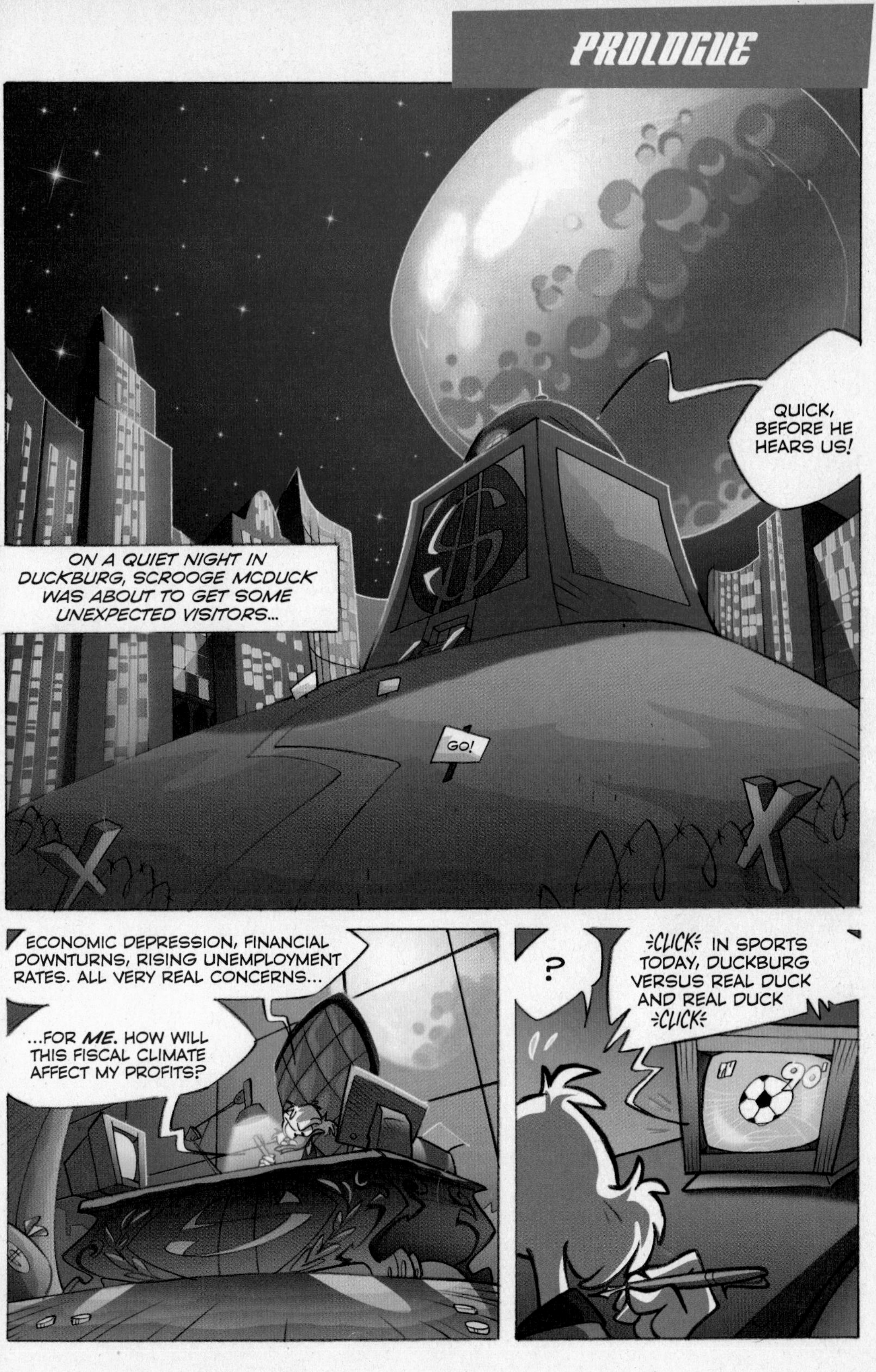
PROLOGUE
ON A QUIET NIGHT IN DUCKBURG, SCROOGE MCDUCK WAS ABOUT TO GET SOME UNEXPECTED VISITORS...
QUICK, BEFORE HE HEARS US!
GO!
ECONOMIC DEPRESSION, FINANCIAL DOWNTURNS, RISING UNEMPLOYMENT RATES. ALL VERY REAL CONCERNS...
...FOR ME. HOW WILL THIS FISCAL CLIMATE AFFECT MY PROFITS?
?
CLICK IN SPORTS TODAY, DUCKBURG VERSUS REAL DUCK AND REAL DUCK CLICK
TV
90'

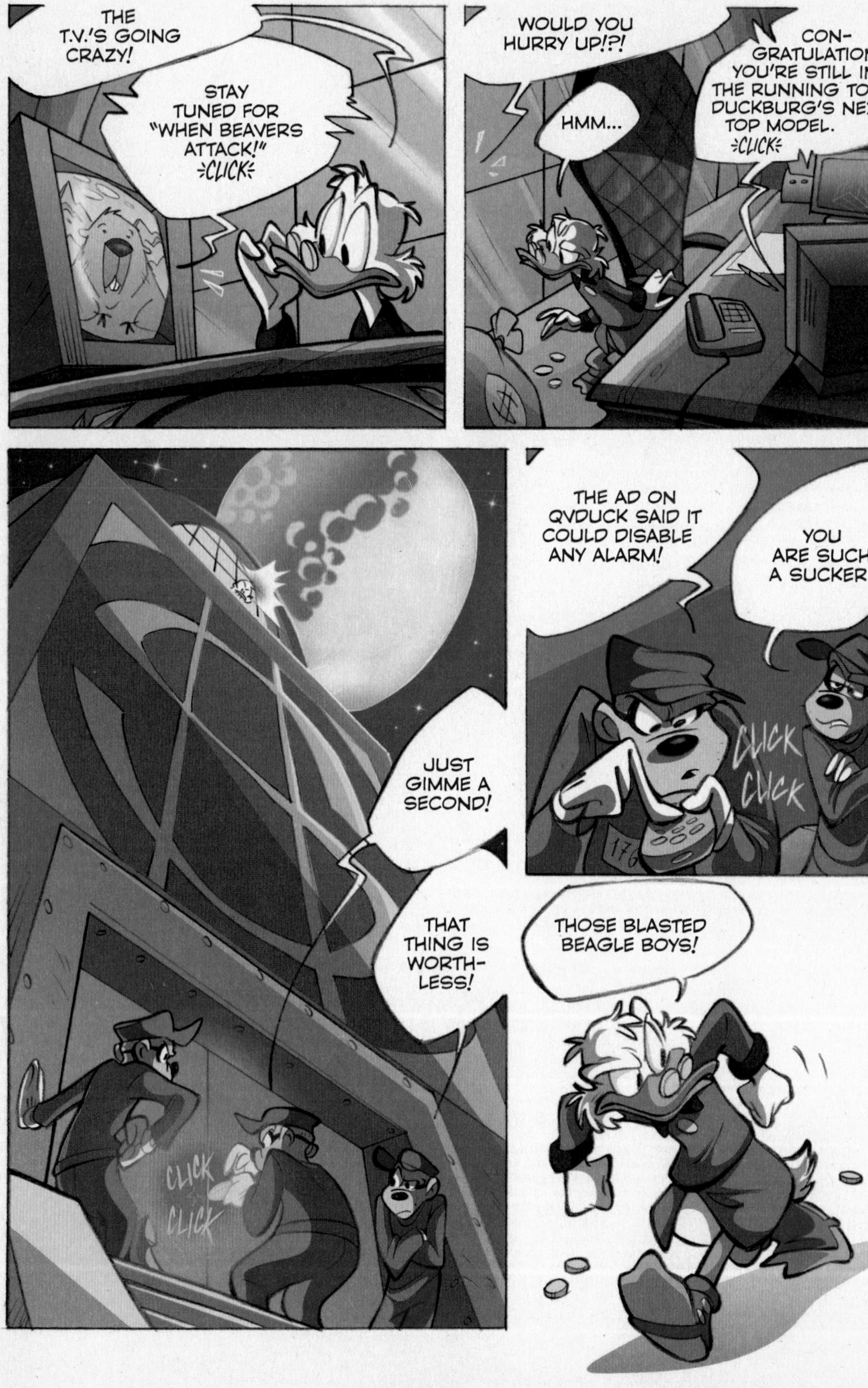
THE T.V.'S GOING CRAZY!
STAY TUNED FOR "WHEN BEAVERS ATTACK!" *CLICK*
WOULD YOU HURRY UP!?!
HMM...
CON-GRATULATIONS. YOU'RE STILL IN THE RUNNING TO BE DUCKBURG'S NEXT TOP MODEL. *CLICK*
JUST GIMME A SECOND!
THAT THING IS WORTH-LESS!
CLICK CLICK
THE AD ON QVDUCK SAID IT COULD DISABLE ANY ALARM!
YOU ARE SUCH A SUCKER.
CLICK CLICK
THOSE BLASTED BEAGLE BOYS!

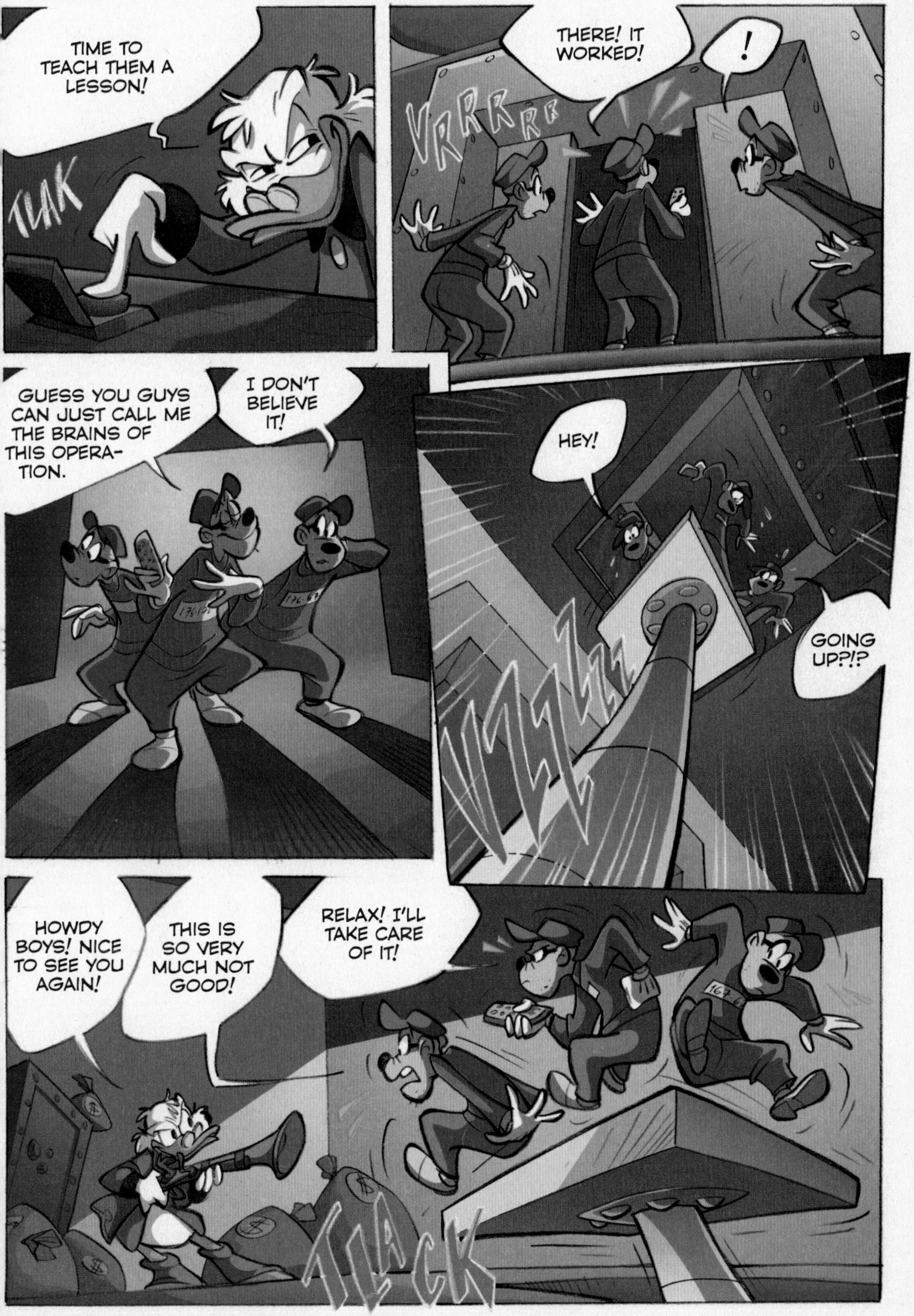
TIME TO TEACH THEM A LESSON!
TLAK
THERE! IT WORKED!
!
VRRRRR
GUESS YOU GUYS CAN JUST CALL ME THE BRAINS OF THIS OPERA-TION.
I DON'T BELIEVE IT!
HEY!
VIZZZZZ
GOING UP?!?
HOWDY BOYS! NICE TO SEE YOU AGAIN!
THIS IS SO VERY MUCH NOT GOOD!
RELAX! I'LL TAKE CARE OF IT!
TLACK

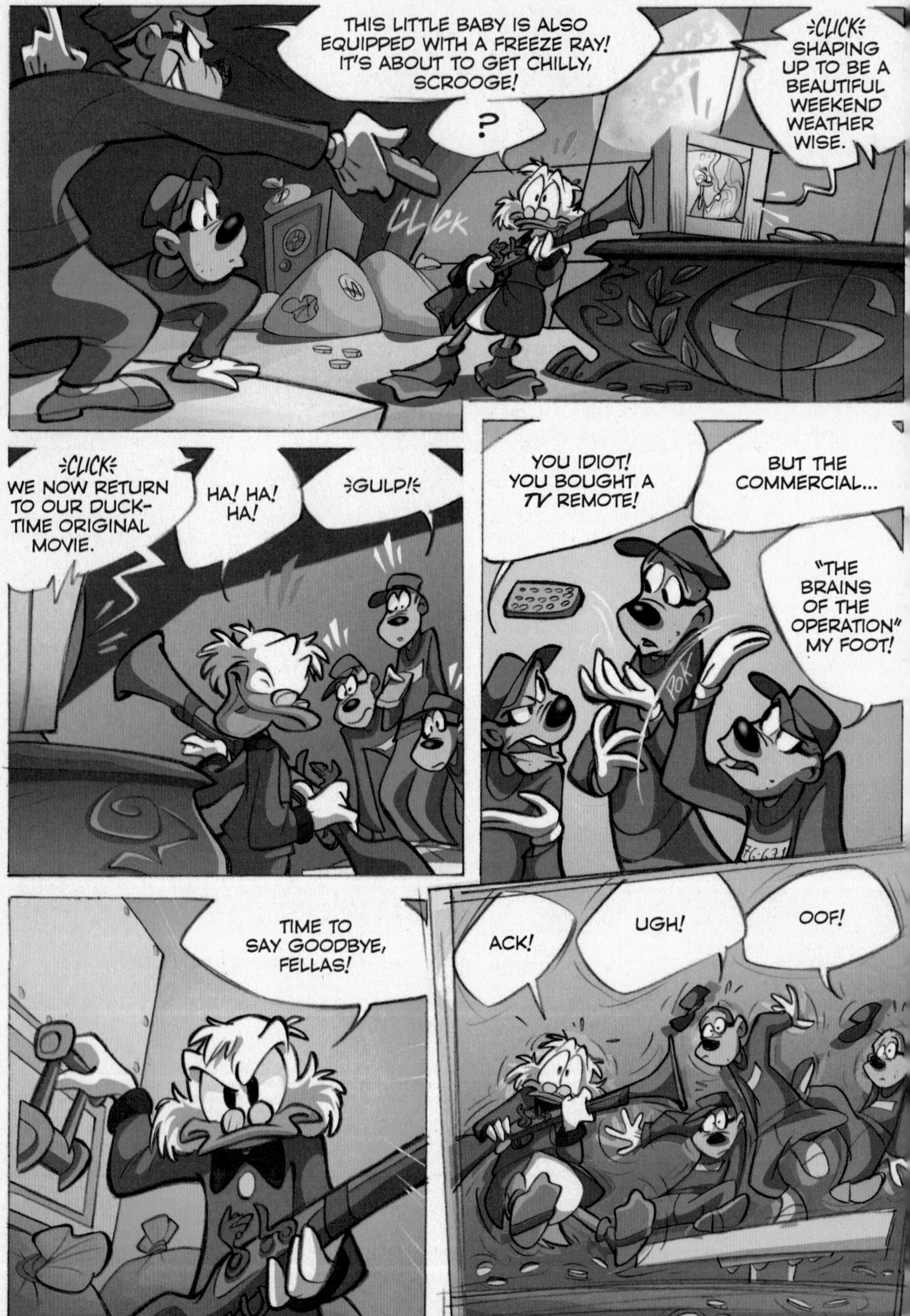
THIS LITTLE BABY IS ALSO EQUIPPED WITH A FREEZE RAY! IT'S ABOUT TO GET CHILLY, SCROOGE!
?
CLICK
⁘CLICK⁘ SHAPING UP TO BE A BEAUTIFUL WEEKEND WEATHER WISE.
⁘CLICK⁘ WE NOW RETURN TO OUR DUCK-TIME ORIGINAL MOVIE.
HA! HA! HA!
⁘GULP!⁘
YOU IDIOT! YOU BOUGHT A *TV* REMOTE!
BUT THE COMMERCIAL...
"THE BRAINS OF THE OPERATION" MY FOOT!
POK
TIME TO SAY GOODBYE, FELLAS!
ACK!
UGH!
OOF!

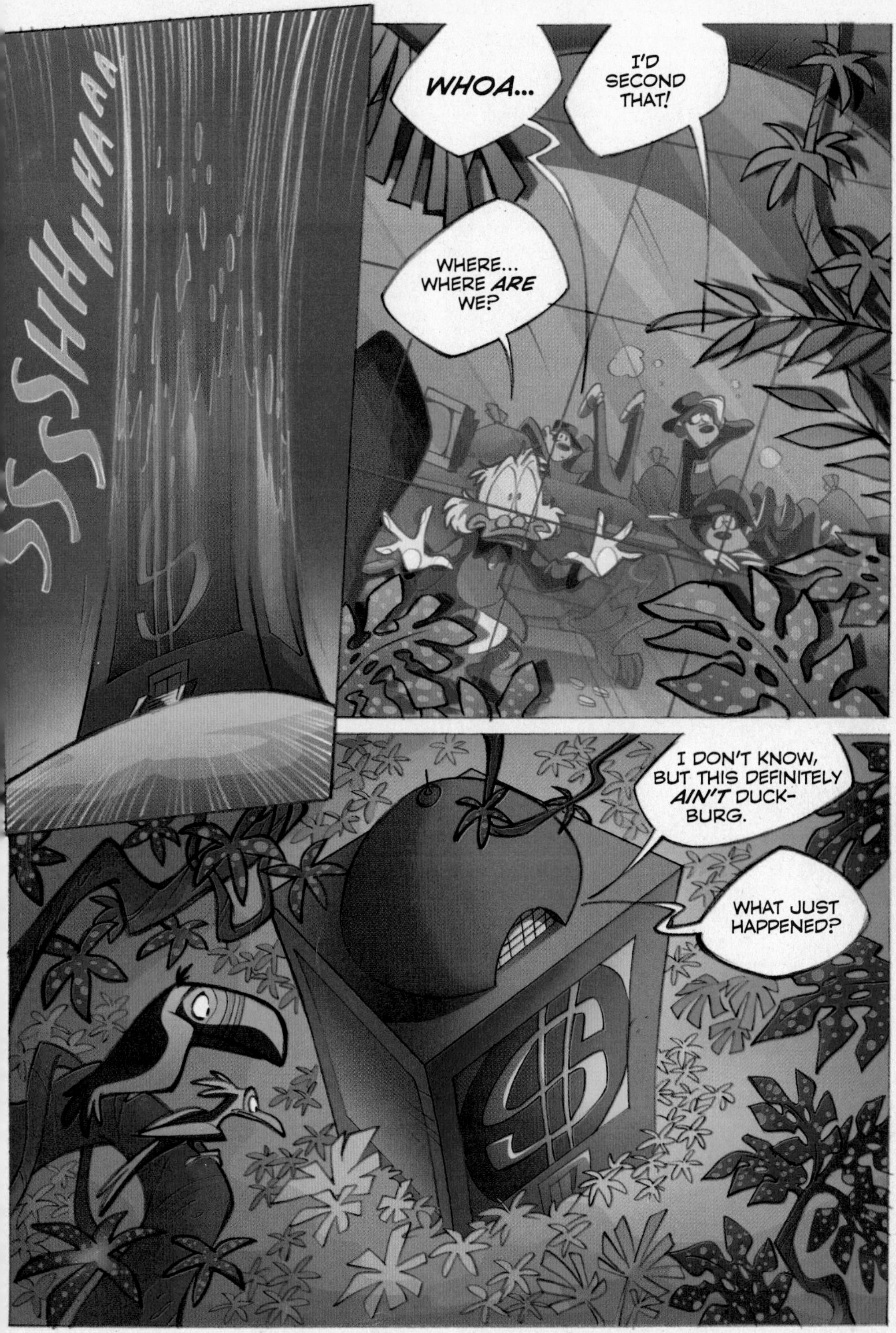
SSSHHHHHAAAA
WHOA...
I'D SECOND THAT!
WHERE... WHERE ARE WE?
I DON'T KNOW, BUT THIS DEFINITELY AIN'T DUCK-BURG.
WHAT JUST HAPPENED?

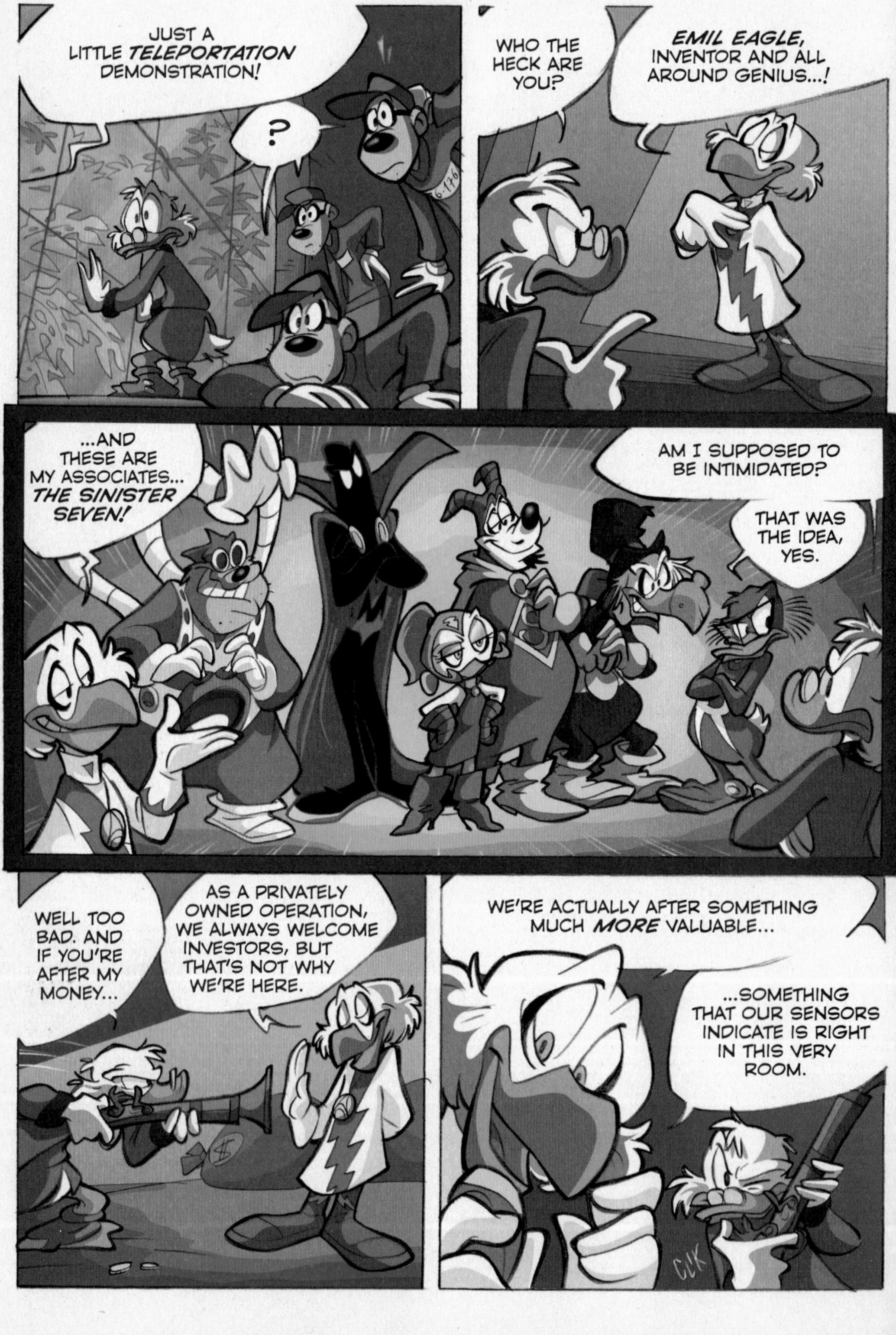
JUST A LITTLE *TELEPORTATION* DEMONSTRATION!
?
6-176
WHO THE HECK ARE YOU?
EMIL EAGLE, INVENTOR AND ALL AROUND GENIUS...!
...AND THESE ARE MY ASSOCIATES... *THE SINISTER SEVEN!*
AM I SUPPOSED TO BE INTIMIDATED?
THAT WAS THE IDEA, YES.
WELL TOO BAD. AND IF YOU'RE AFTER MY MONEY...
AS A PRIVATELY OWNED OPERATION, WE ALWAYS WELCOME INVESTORS, BUT THAT'S NOT WHY WE'RE HERE.
WE'RE ACTUALLY AFTER SOMETHING MUCH *MORE* VALUABLE...
...SOMETHING THAT OUR SENSORS INDICATE IS RIGHT IN THIS VERY ROOM.
CLIK

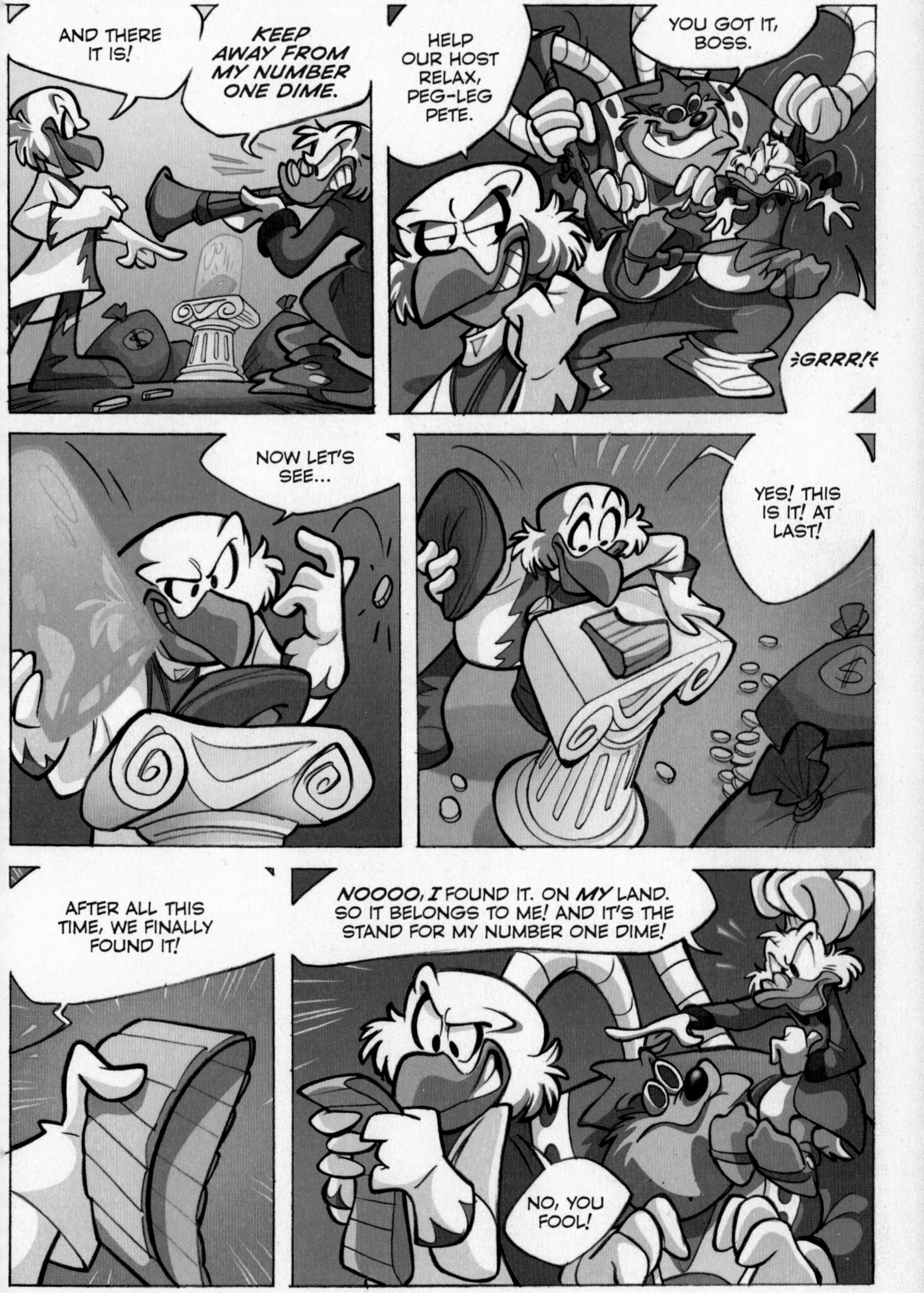
AND THERE IT IS!
KEEP AWAY FROM MY NUMBER ONE DIME.
HELP OUR HOST RELAX, PEG-LEG PETE.
YOU GOT IT, BOSS.
GRRR!
NOW LET'S SEE...
YES! THIS IS IT! AT LAST!
AFTER ALL THIS TIME, WE FINALLY FOUND IT!
NOOOO, I FOUND IT. ON MY LAND. SO IT BELONGS TO ME! AND IT'S THE STAND FOR MY NUMBER ONE DIME!
NO, YOU FOOL!

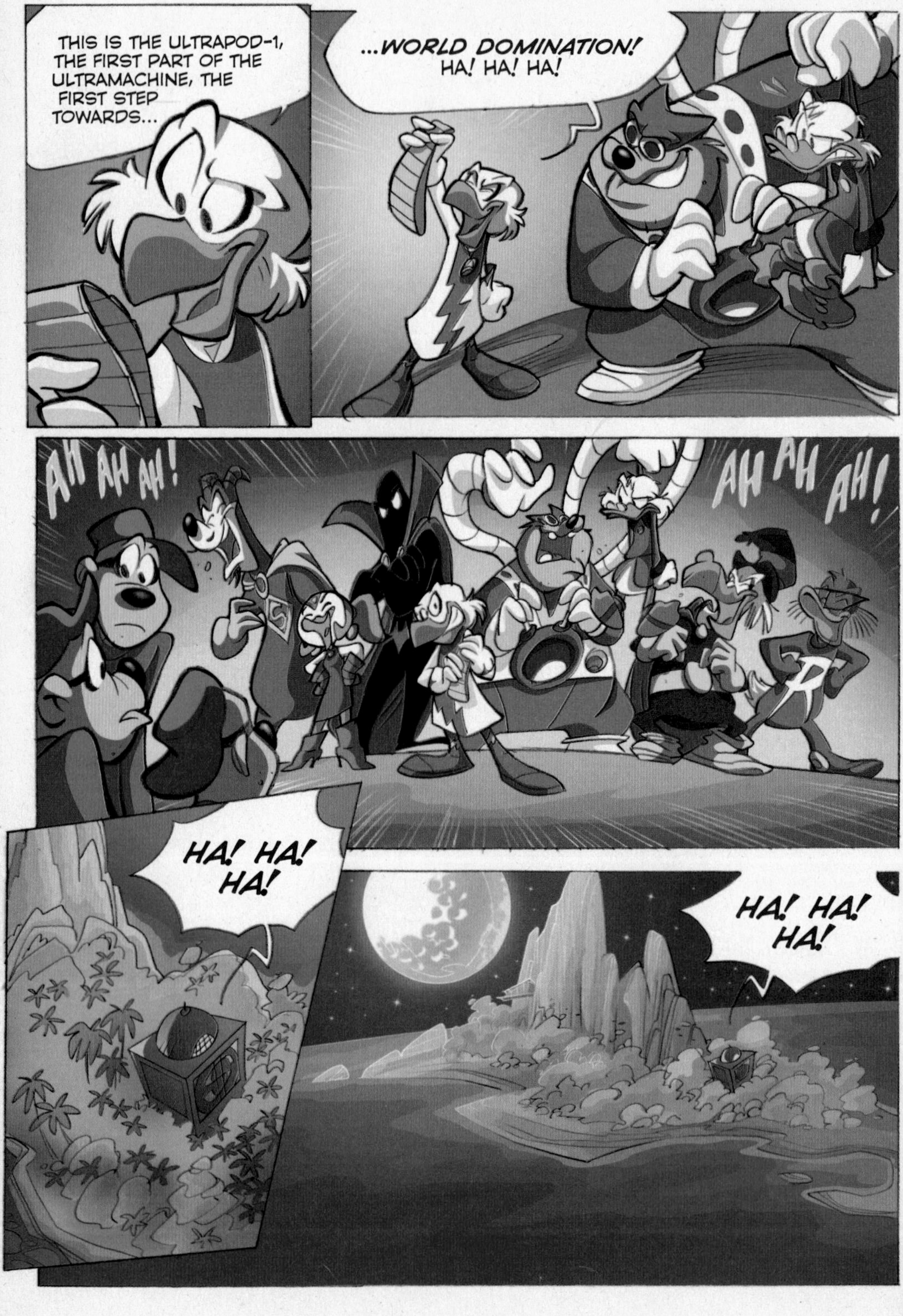
THIS IS THE ULTRAPOD-1, THE FIRST PART OF THE ULTRAMACHINE, THE FIRST STEP TOWARDS...
...WORLD DOMINATION! HA! HA! HA!
AH AH AH!
AH AH AH AH!
HA! HA! HA!
HA! HA! HA!

CHAPTER ONE

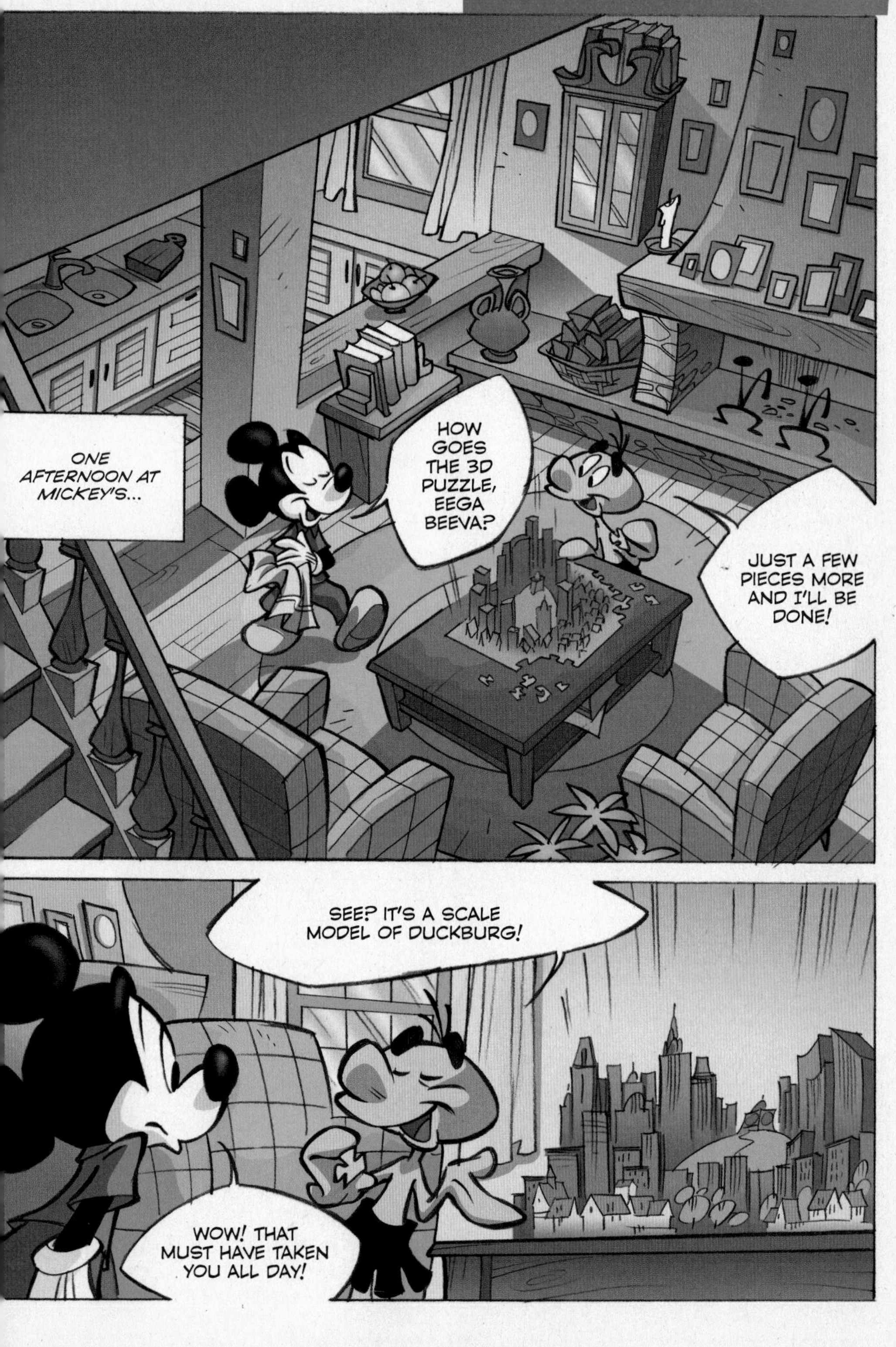

ONE AFTERNOON AT MICKEY'S...
HOW GOES THE 3D PUZZLE, EEGA BEEVA?
JUST A FEW PIECES MORE AND I'LL BE DONE!
SEE? IT'S A SCALE MODEL OF DUCKBURG!
WOW! THAT MUST HAVE TAKEN YOU ALL DAY!

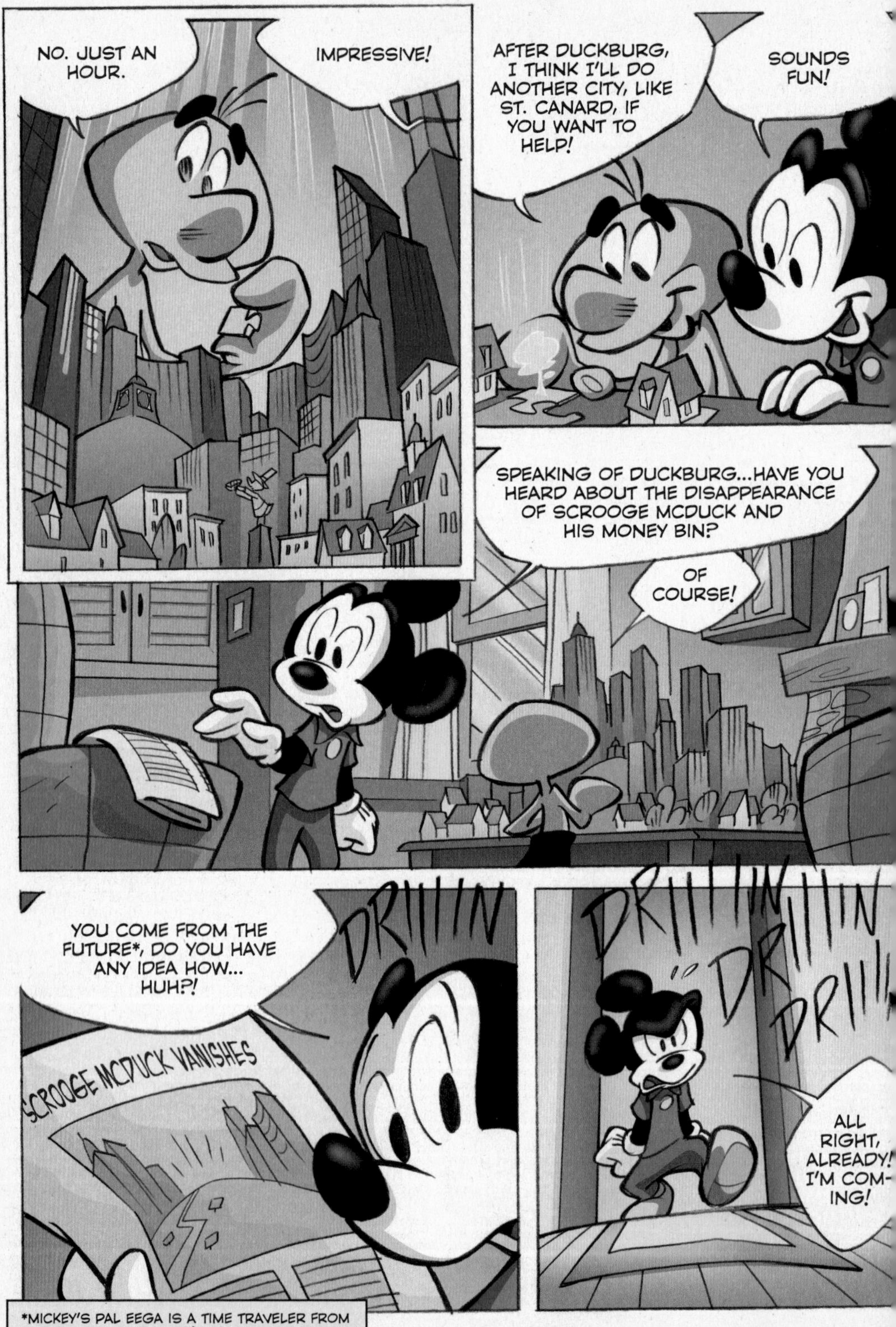
NO. JUST AN HOUR.
IMPRESSIVE!
AFTER DUCKBURG, I THINK I'LL DO ANOTHER CITY, LIKE ST. CANARD, IF YOU WANT TO HELP!
SOUNDS FUN!
SPEAKING OF DUCKBURG...HAVE YOU HEARD ABOUT THE DISAPPEARANCE OF SCROOGE MCDUCK AND HIS MONEY BIN?
OF COURSE!
YOU COME FROM THE FUTURE*, DO YOU HAVE ANY IDEA HOW... HUH?!
DRIIIIN
SCROOGE MCDUCK VANISHES
DRIIIIN
DRIIIIN
DRIIII
DRIIII
ALL RIGHT, ALREADY! I'M COMING!

*MICKEY'S PAL EEGA IS A TIME TRAVELER FROM THE FAR-FLUNG FUTURE! – FUTURISTIC AARON

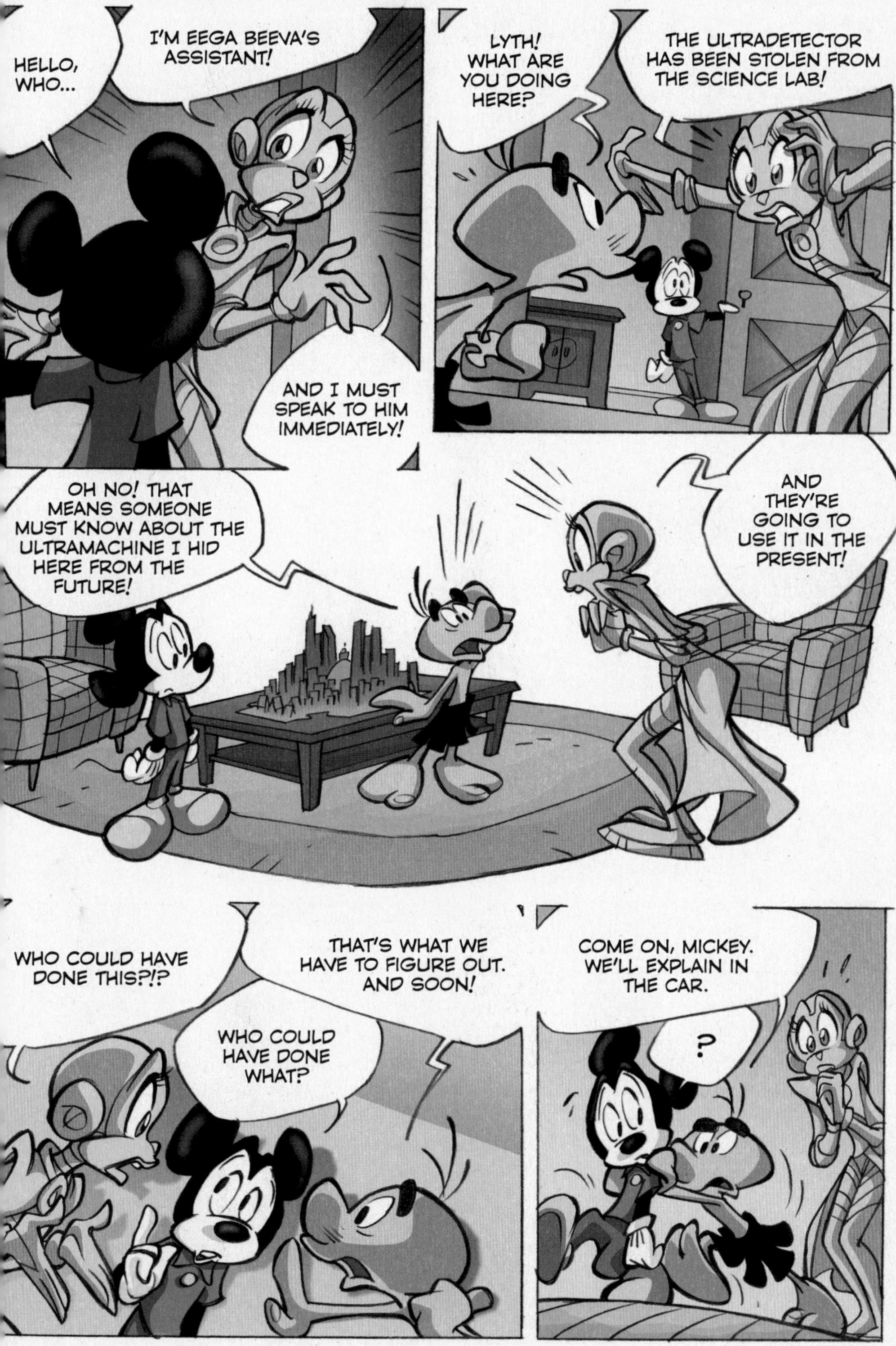
HELLO, WHO...
I'M EEGA BEEVA'S ASSISTANT!
AND I MUST SPEAK TO HIM IMMEDIATELY!
LYTH! WHAT ARE YOU DOING HERE?
THE ULTRADETECTOR HAS BEEN STOLEN FROM THE SCIENCE LAB!
OH NO! THAT MEANS SOMEONE MUST KNOW ABOUT THE ULTRAMACHINE I HID HERE FROM THE FUTURE!
AND THEY'RE GOING TO USE IT IN THE PRESENT!
WHO COULD HAVE DONE THIS?!?
WHO COULD HAVE DONE WHAT?
THAT'S WHAT WE HAVE TO FIGURE OUT. AND SOON!
COME ON, MICKEY. WE'LL EXPLAIN IN THE CAR.
?

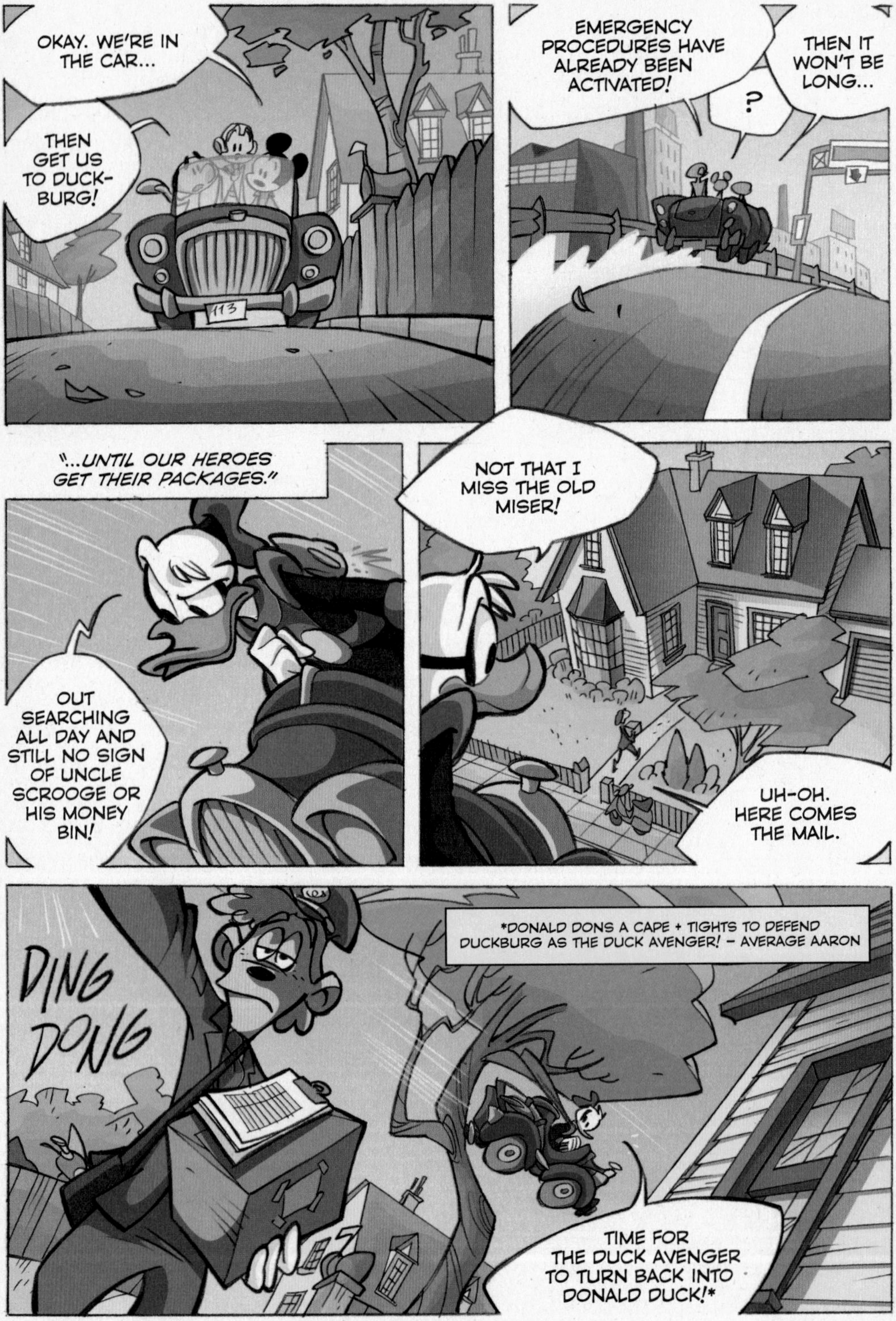
OKAY. WE'RE IN THE CAR...
THEN GET US TO DUCK-BURG!
EMERGENCY PROCEDURES HAVE ALREADY BEEN ACTIVATED!
?
THEN IT WON'T BE LONG...
"...UNTIL OUR HEROES GET THEIR PACKAGES."
OUT SEARCHING ALL DAY AND STILL NO SIGN OF UNCLE SCROOGE OR HIS MONEY BIN!
NOT THAT I MISS THE OLD MISER!
UH-OH. HERE COMES THE MAIL.
*DONALD DONS A CAPE + TIGHTS TO DEFEND DUCKBURG AS THE DUCK AVENGER! – AVERAGE AARON
DING DONG
TIME FOR THE DUCK AVENGER TO TURN BACK INTO DONALD DUCK!*

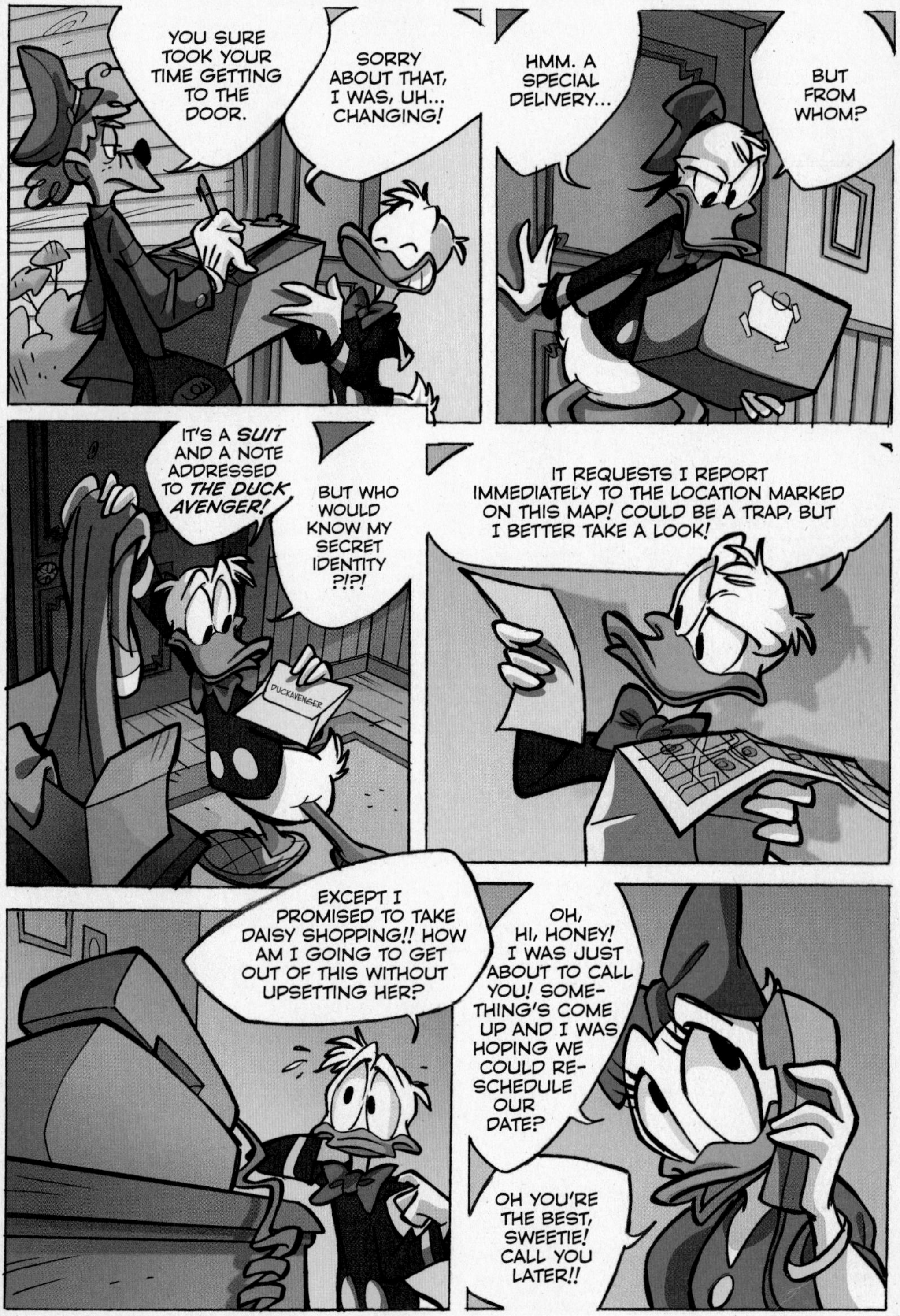
YOU SURE TOOK YOUR TIME GETTING TO THE DOOR.
SORRY ABOUT THAT, I WAS, UH... CHANGING!
HMM. A SPECIAL DELIVERY...
BUT FROM WHOM?
IT'S A SUIT AND A NOTE ADDRESSED TO THE DUCK AVENGER!
BUT WHO WOULD KNOW MY SECRET IDENTITY ?!?!
DUCKAVENGER
IT REQUESTS I REPORT IMMEDIATELY TO THE LOCATION MARKED ON THIS MAP! COULD BE A TRAP, BUT I BETTER TAKE A LOOK!
EXCEPT I PROMISED TO TAKE DAISY SHOPPING!! HOW AM I GOING TO GET OUT OF THIS WITHOUT UPSETTING HER?
OH, HI, HONEY! I WAS JUST ABOUT TO CALL YOU! SOME-THING'S COME UP AND I WAS HOPING WE COULD RE-SCHEDULE OUR DATE?
OH YOU'RE THE BEST, SWEETIE! CALL YOU LATER!!

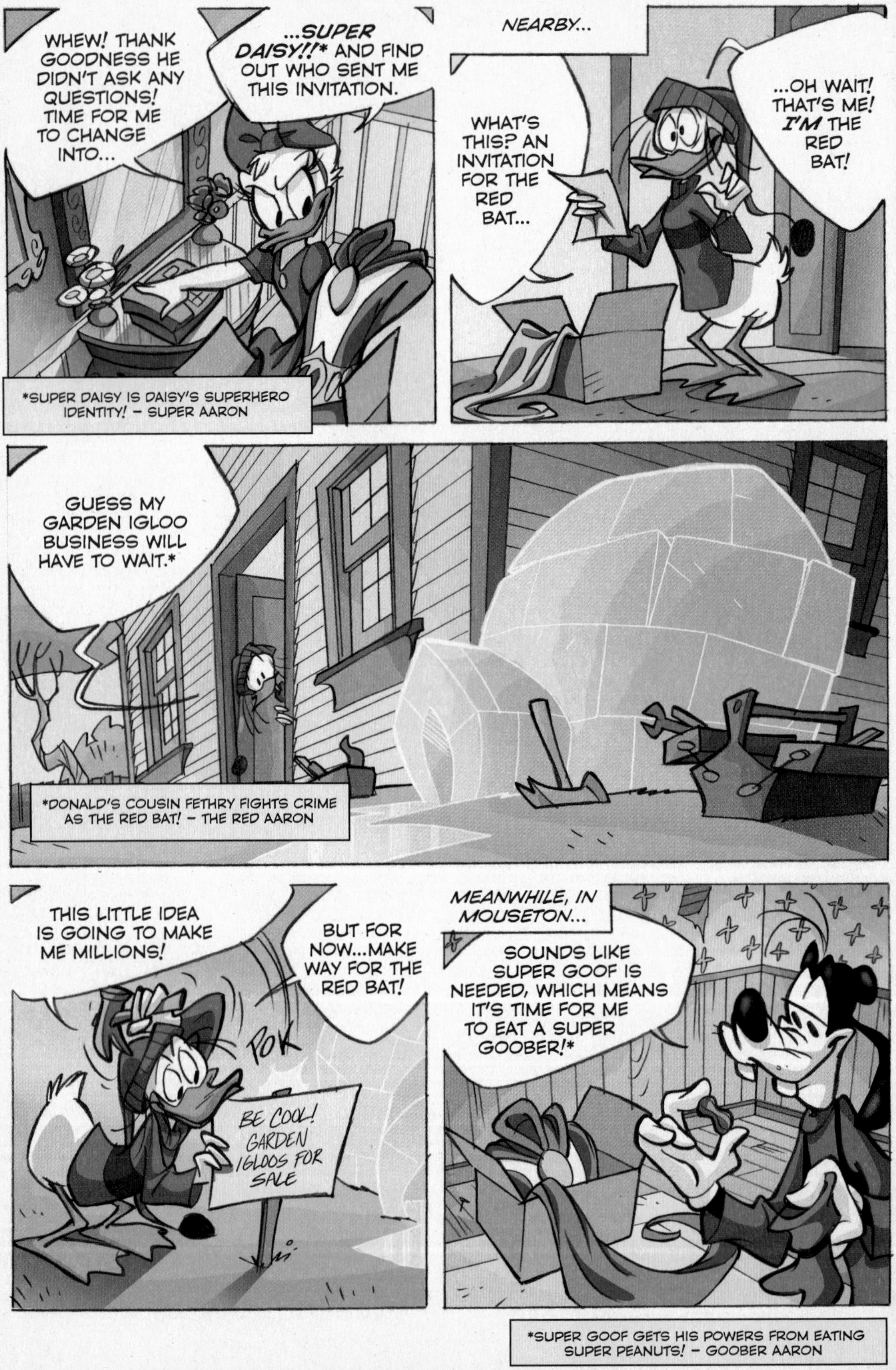

WHEW! THANK GOODNESS HE DIDN'T ASK ANY QUESTIONS! TIME FOR ME TO CHANGE INTO...
...SUPER DAISY!!* AND FIND OUT WHO SENT ME THIS INVITATION.
*SUPER DAISY IS DAISY'S SUPERHERO IDENTITY! – SUPER AARON
NEARBY...
WHAT'S THIS? AN INVITATION FOR THE RED BAT...
...OH WAIT! THAT'S ME! I'M THE RED BAT!
GUESS MY GARDEN IGLOO BUSINESS WILL HAVE TO WAIT.*
*DONALD'S COUSIN FETHRY FIGHTS CRIME AS THE RED BAT! – THE RED AARON
THIS LITTLE IDEA IS GOING TO MAKE ME MILLIONS!
BUT FOR NOW...MAKE WAY FOR THE RED BAT!
POK
BE COOL! GARDEN IGLOOS FOR SALE
MEANWHILE, IN MOUSETON...
SOUNDS LIKE SUPER GOOF IS NEEDED, WHICH MEANS IT'S TIME FOR ME TO EAT A SUPER GOOBER!*
*SUPER GOOF GETS HIS POWERS FROM EATING SUPER PEANUTS! – GOOBER AARON

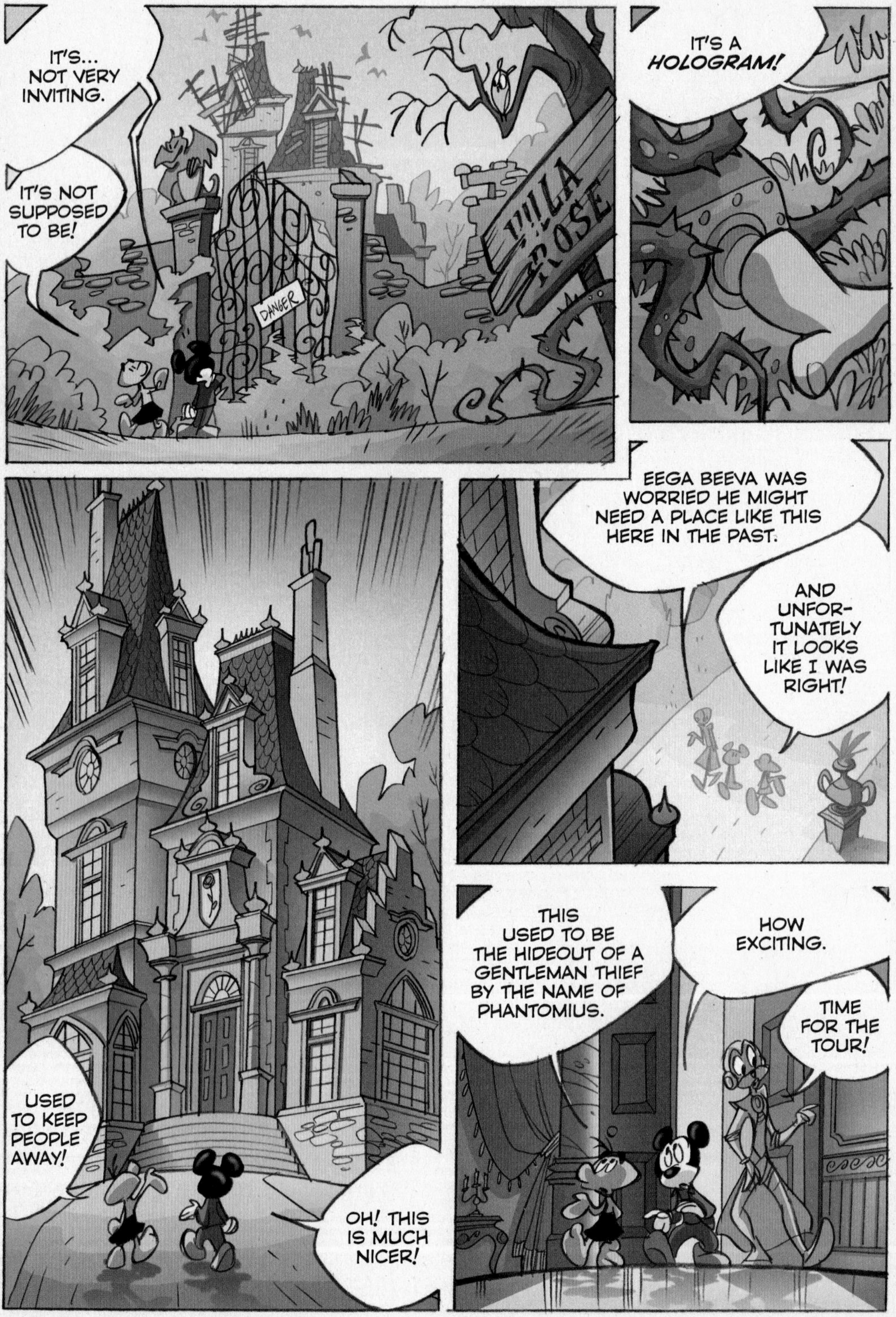
IT'S... NOT VERY INVITING.
IT'S NOT SUPPOSED TO BE!
VILLA ROSE
DANGER
IT'S A HOLOGRAM!
EEGA BEEVA WAS WORRIED HE MIGHT NEED A PLACE LIKE THIS HERE IN THE PAST.
AND UNFOR-TUNATELY IT LOOKS LIKE I WAS RIGHT!
USED TO KEEP PEOPLE AWAY!
OH! THIS IS MUCH NICER!
THIS USED TO BE THE HIDEOUT OF A GENTLEMAN THIEF BY THE NAME OF PHANTOMIUS.
HOW EXCITING.
TIME FOR THE TOUR!

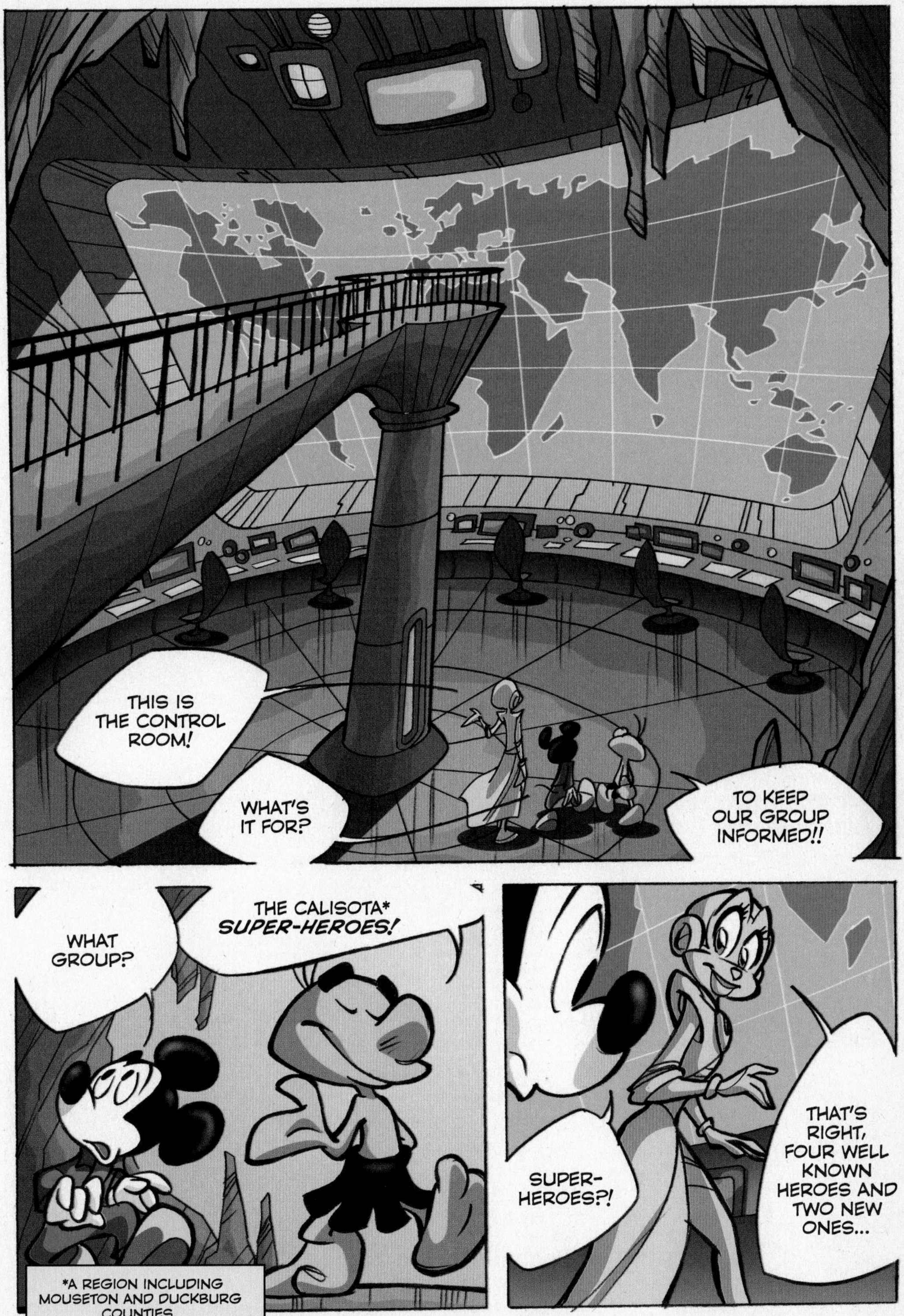
THIS IS THE CONTROL ROOM!
WHAT'S IT FOR?
TO KEEP OUR GROUP INFORMED!!
WHAT GROUP?
THE CALISOTA* SUPER-HEROES!
*A REGION INCLUDING MOUSETON AND DUCKBURG COUNTIES.
SUPER-HEROES?!
THAT'S RIGHT, FOUR WELL KNOWN HEROES AND TWO NEW ONES...

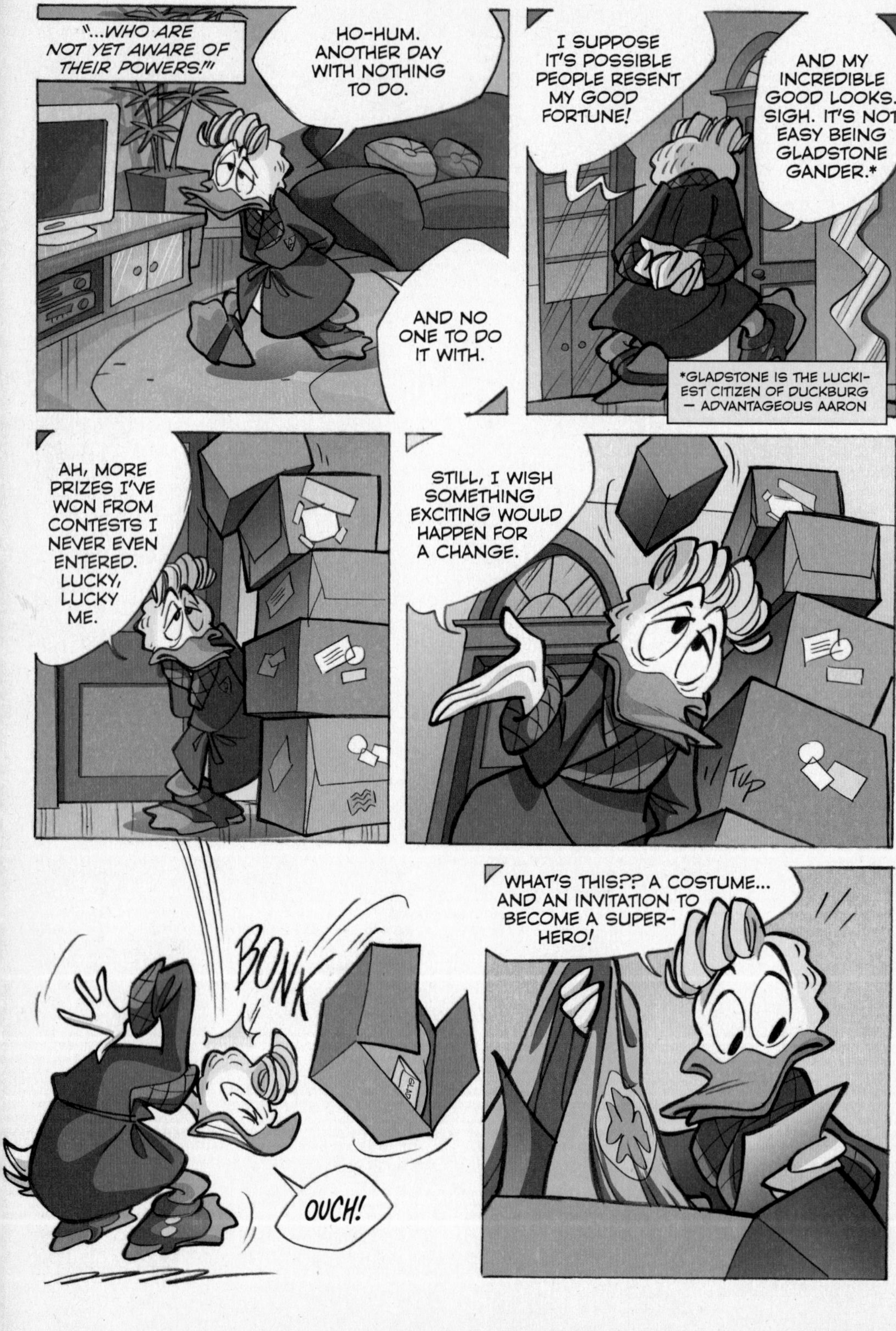
"...WHO ARE NOT YET AWARE OF THEIR POWERS!"
HO-HUM. ANOTHER DAY WITH NOTHING TO DO.
AND NO ONE TO DO IT WITH.
I SUPPOSE IT'S POSSIBLE PEOPLE RESENT MY GOOD FORTUNE!
AND MY INCREDIBLE GOOD LOOKS. SIGH. IT'S NOT EASY BEING GLADSTONE GANDER.*
*GLADSTONE IS THE LUCKIEST CITIZEN OF DUCKBURG — ADVANTAGEOUS AARON
AH, MORE PRIZES I'VE WON FROM CONTESTS I NEVER EVEN ENTERED. LUCKY, LUCKY ME.
STILL, I WISH SOMETHING EXCITING WOULD HAPPEN FOR A CHANGE.
BONK
OUCH!
WHAT'S THIS?? A COSTUME... AND AN INVITATION TO BECOME A SUPER-HERO!

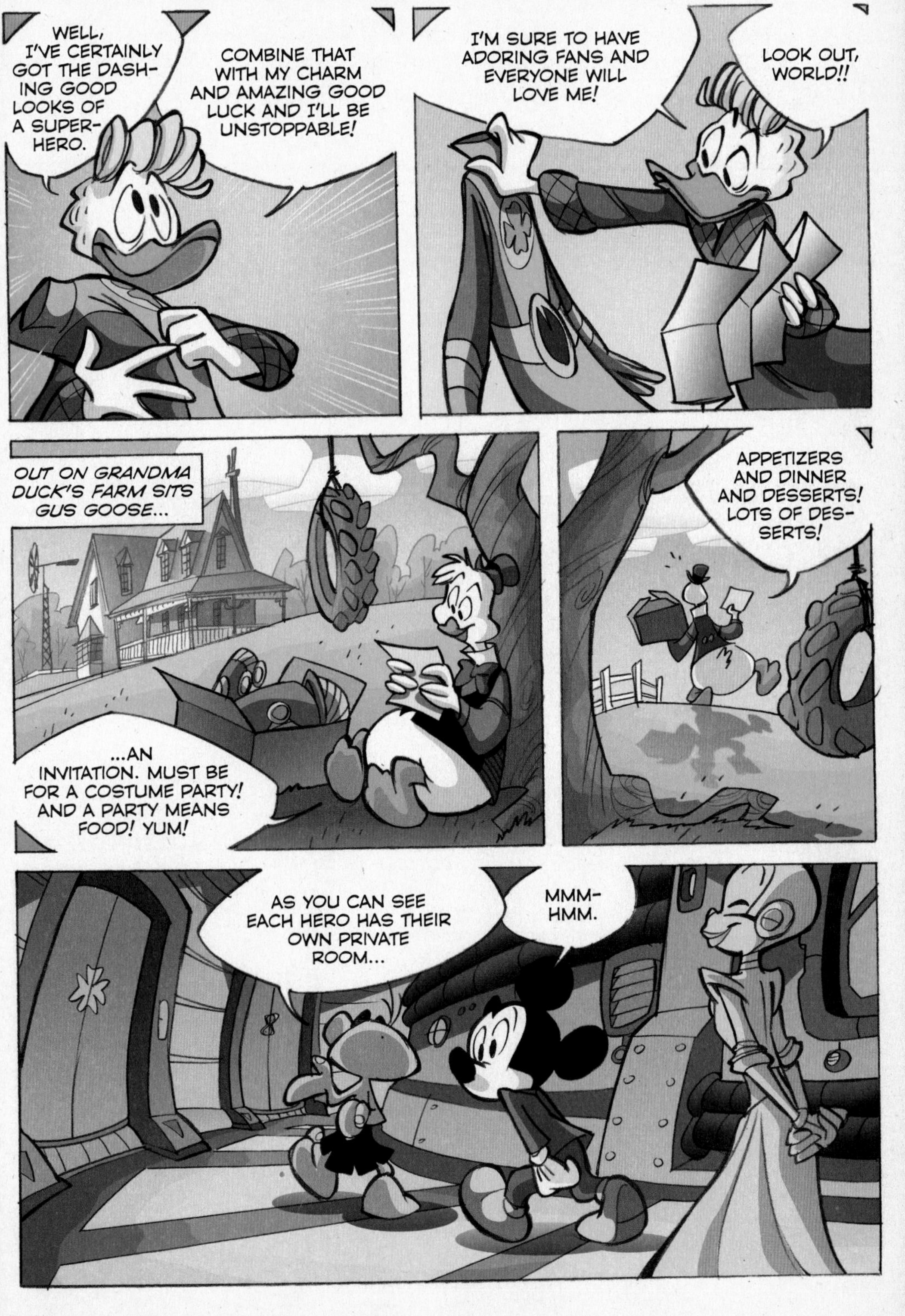

WELL, I'VE CERTAINLY GOT THE DASHING GOOD LOOKS OF A SUPER-HERO.
COMBINE THAT WITH MY CHARM AND AMAZING GOOD LUCK AND I'LL BE UNSTOPPABLE!
I'M SURE TO HAVE ADORING FANS AND EVERYONE WILL LOVE ME!
LOOK OUT, WORLD!!
OUT ON GRANDMA DUCK'S FARM SITS GUS GOOSE...
...AN INVITATION. MUST BE FOR A COSTUME PARTY! AND A PARTY MEANS FOOD! YUM!
APPETIZERS AND DINNER AND DESSERTS! LOTS OF DES-SERTS!
AS YOU CAN SEE EACH HERO HAS THEIR OWN PRIVATE ROOM...
MMM-HMM.

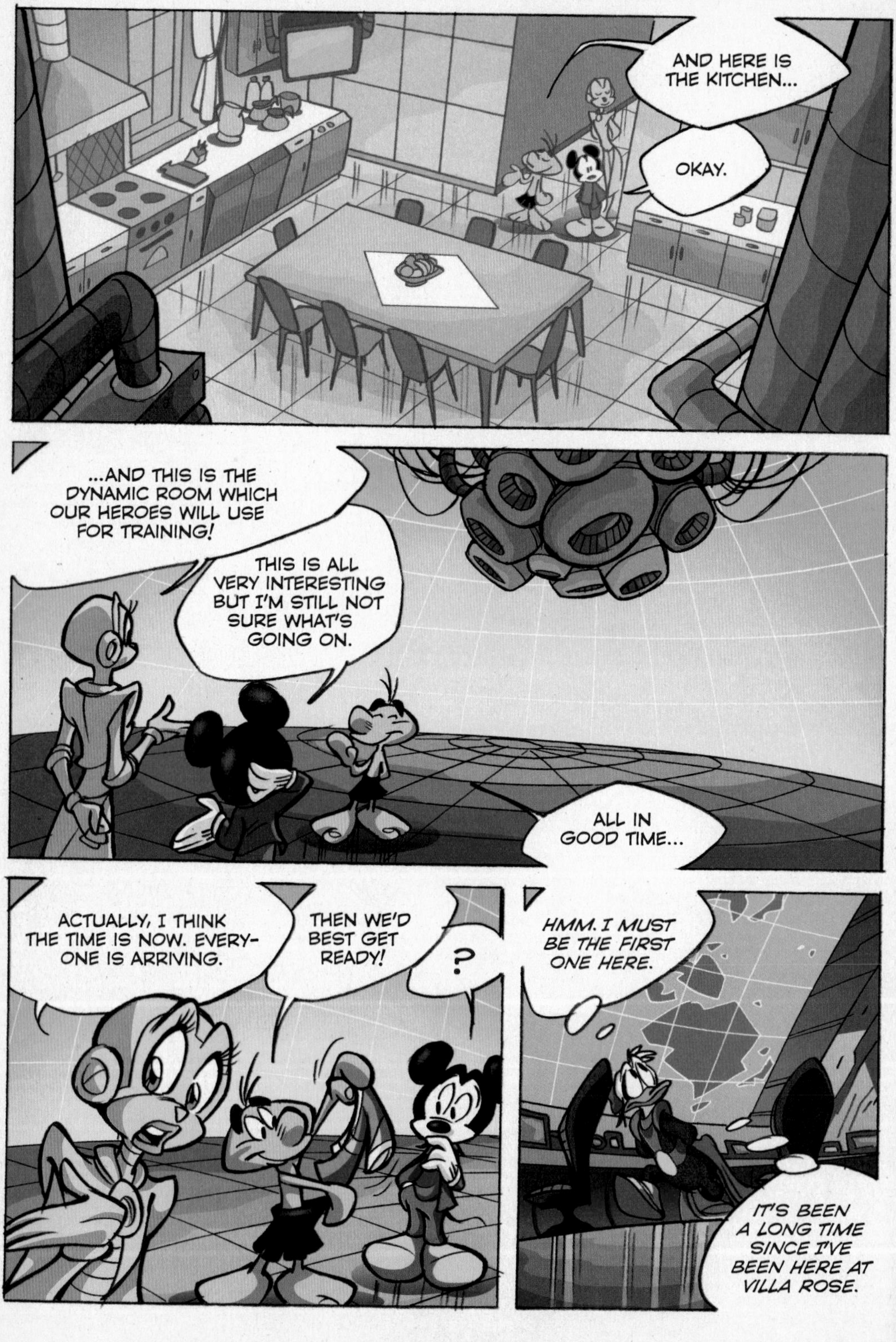
AND HERE IS THE KITCHEN...
OKAY.
...AND THIS IS THE DYNAMIC ROOM WHICH OUR HEROES WILL USE FOR TRAINING!
THIS IS ALL VERY INTERESTING BUT I'M STILL NOT SURE WHAT'S GOING ON.
ALL IN GOOD TIME...
ACTUALLY, I THINK THE TIME IS NOW. EVERY-ONE IS ARRIVING.
THEN WE'D BEST GET READY!
?
HMM. I MUST BE THE FIRST ONE HERE.
IT'S BEEN A LONG TIME SINCE I'VE BEEN HERE AT VILLA ROSE.

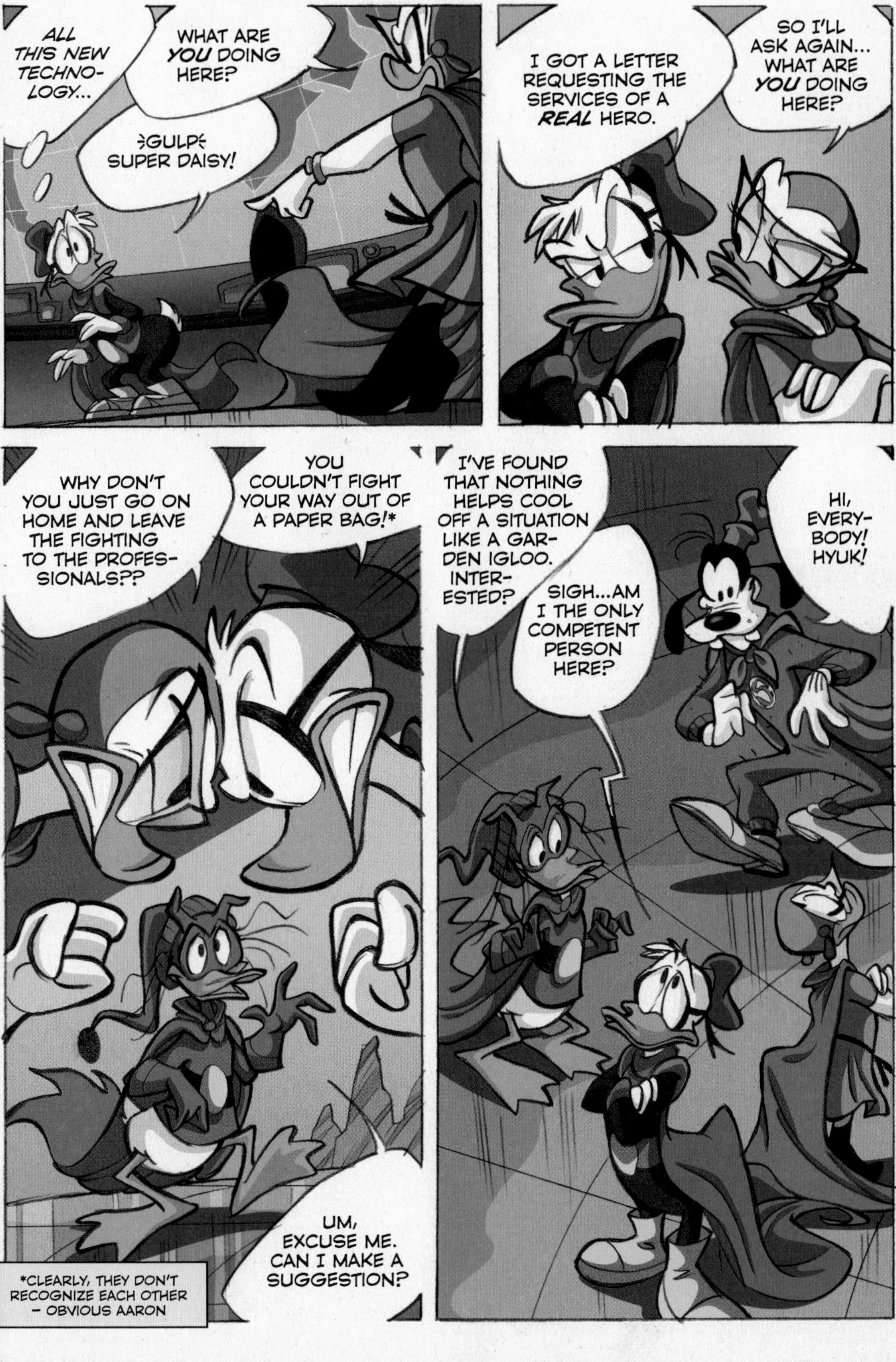
ALL THIS NEW TECHNO-LOGY...
WHAT ARE YOU DOING HERE?
>GULP< SUPER DAISY!
I GOT A LETTER REQUESTING THE SERVICES OF A REAL HERO.
SO I'LL ASK AGAIN... WHAT ARE YOU DOING HERE?
WHY DON'T YOU JUST GO ON HOME AND LEAVE THE FIGHTING TO THE PROFES-SIONALS??
YOU COULDN'T FIGHT YOUR WAY OUT OF A PAPER BAG!*
UM, EXCUSE ME. CAN I MAKE A SUGGESTION?
*CLEARLY, THEY DON'T RECOGNIZE EACH OTHER – OBVIOUS AARON
I'VE FOUND THAT NOTHING HELPS COOL OFF A SITUATION LIKE A GAR-DEN IGLOO. INTER-ESTED?
HI, EVERY-BODY! HYUK!
SIGH...AM I THE ONLY COMPETENT PERSON HERE?

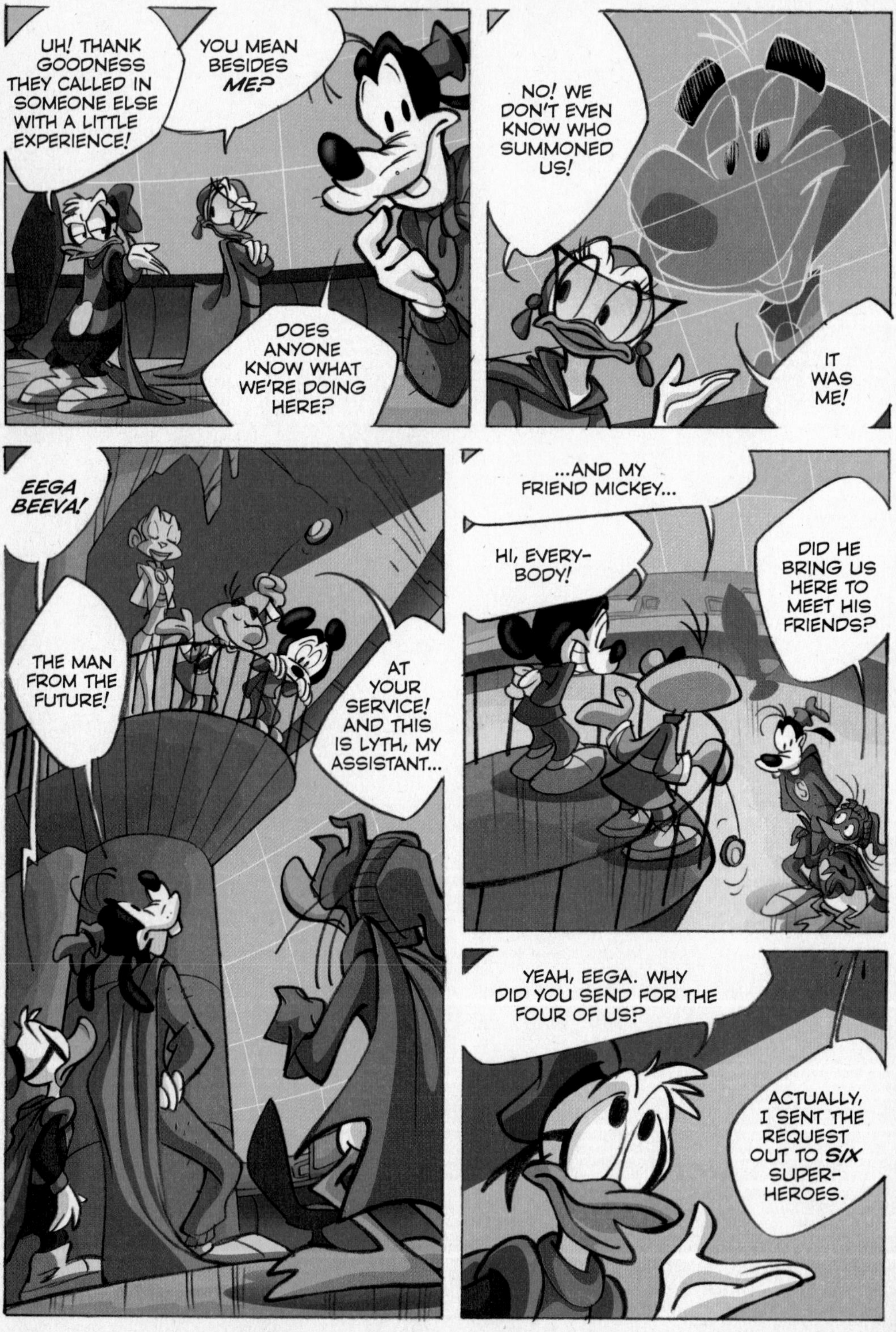
UH! THANK GOODNESS THEY CALLED IN SOMEONE ELSE WITH A LITTLE EXPERIENCE!
YOU MEAN BESIDES *ME?*
DOES ANYONE KNOW WHAT WE'RE DOING HERE?
NO! WE DON'T EVEN KNOW WHO SUMMONED US!
IT WAS ME!
EEGA BEEVA!
THE MAN FROM THE FUTURE!
AT YOUR SERVICE! AND THIS IS LYTH, MY ASSISTANT...
...AND MY FRIEND MICKEY...
HI, EVERY-BODY!
DID HE BRING US HERE TO MEET HIS FRIENDS?
YEAH, EEGA. WHY DID YOU SEND FOR THE FOUR OF US?
ACTUALLY, I SENT THE REQUEST OUT TO *SIX* SUPER-HEROES.

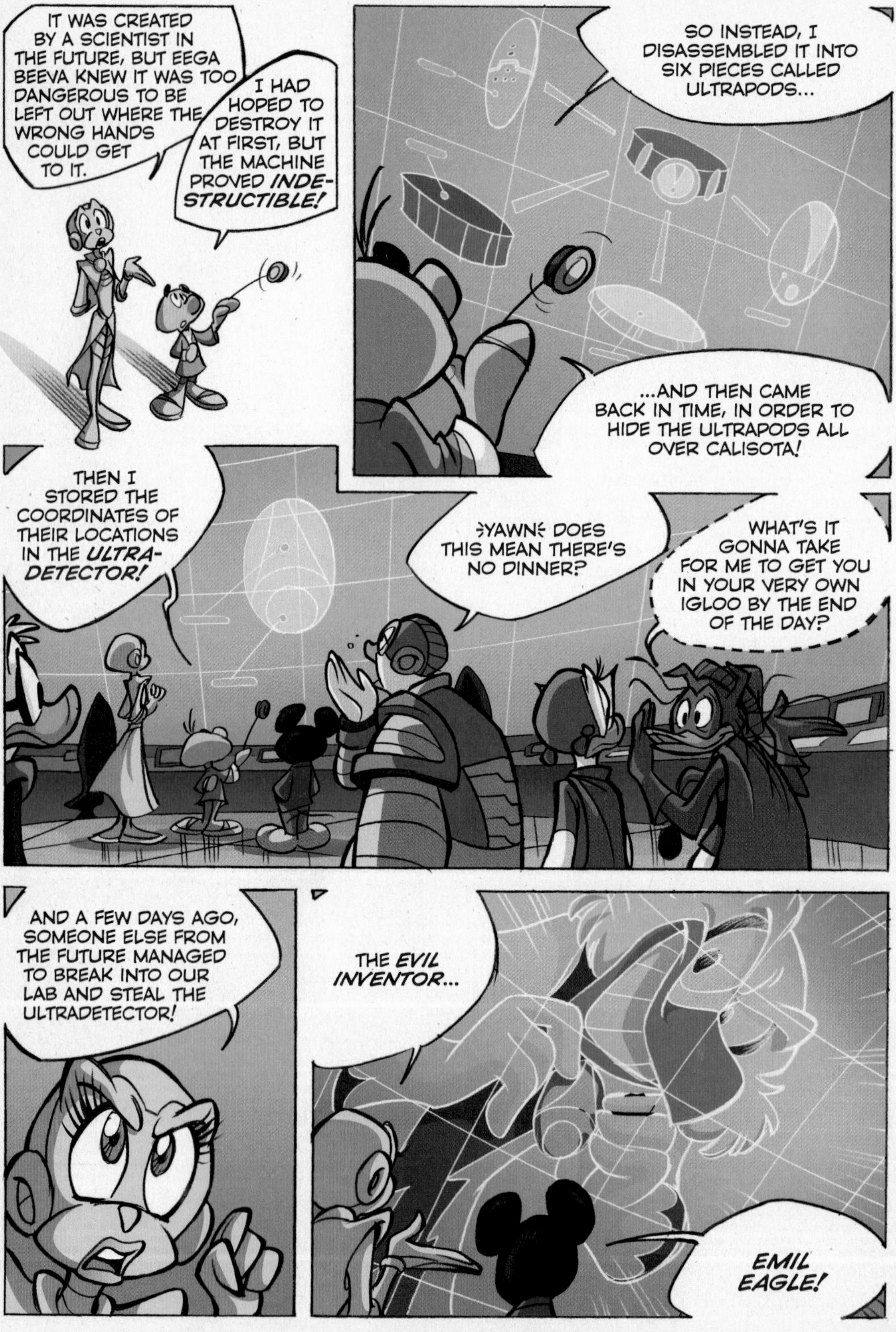
IT WAS CREATED BY A SCIENTIST IN THE FUTURE, BUT EEGA BEEVA KNEW IT WAS TOO DANGEROUS TO BE LEFT OUT WHERE THE WRONG HANDS COULD GET TO IT.
I HAD HOPED TO DESTROY IT AT FIRST, BUT THE MACHINE PROVED INDESTRUCTIBLE!
SO INSTEAD, I DISASSEMBLED IT INTO SIX PIECES CALLED ULTRAPODS...
...AND THEN CAME BACK IN TIME, IN ORDER TO HIDE THE ULTRAPODS ALL OVER CALISOTA!
THEN I STORED THE COORDINATES OF THEIR LOCATIONS IN THE ULTRA-DETECTOR!
YAWN DOES THIS MEAN THERE'S NO DINNER?
WHAT'S IT GONNA TAKE FOR ME TO GET YOU IN YOUR VERY OWN IGLOO BY THE END OF THE DAY?
AND A FEW DAYS AGO, SOMEONE ELSE FROM THE FUTURE MANAGED TO BREAK INTO OUR LAB AND STEAL THE ULTRADETECTOR!
THE EVIL INVENTOR...
EMIL EAGLE!

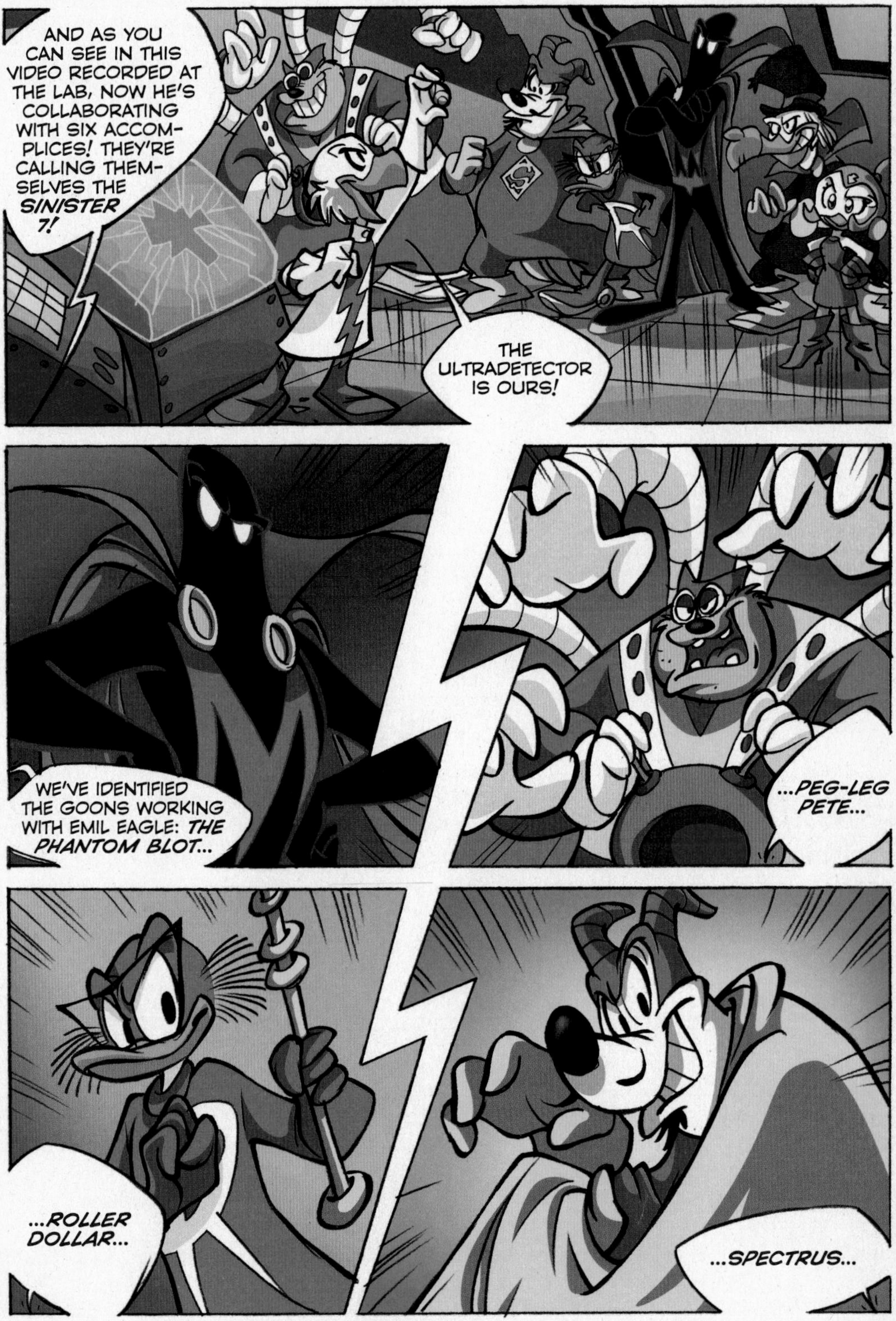
AND AS YOU CAN SEE IN THIS VIDEO RECORDED AT THE LAB, NOW HE'S COLLABORATING WITH SIX ACCOMPLICES! THEY'RE CALLING THEMSELVES THE *SINISTER 7!*
THE ULTRADETECTOR IS OURS!
WE'VE IDENTIFIED THE GOONS WORKING WITH EMIL EAGLE: *THE PHANTOM BLOT...*
...PEG-LEG PETE...
...ROLLER DOLLAR...
...SPECTRUS...

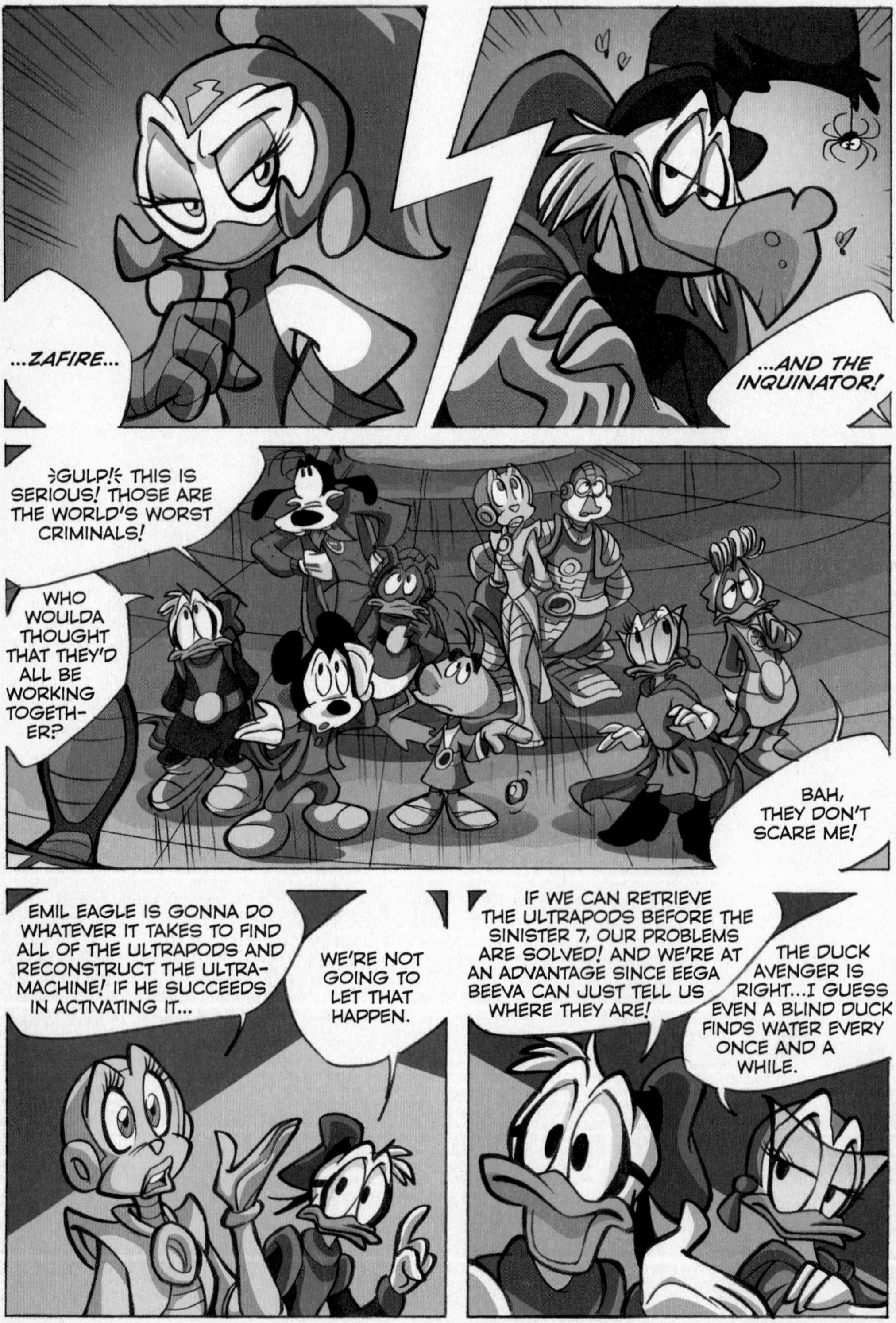
...ZAFIRE...
...AND THE INQUINATOR!
⊰GULP!⊱ THIS IS SERIOUS! THOSE ARE THE WORLD'S WORST CRIMINALS!
WHO WOULDA THOUGHT THAT THEY'D ALL BE WORKING TOGETH-ER?
BAH, THEY DON'T SCARE ME!
EMIL EAGLE IS GONNA DO WHATEVER IT TAKES TO FIND ALL OF THE ULTRAPODS AND RECONSTRUCT THE ULTRA-MACHINE! IF HE SUCCEEDS IN ACTIVATING IT...
WE'RE NOT GOING TO LET THAT HAPPEN.
IF WE CAN RETRIEVE THE ULTRAPODS BEFORE THE SINISTER 7, OUR PROBLEMS ARE SOLVED! AND WE'RE AT AN ADVANTAGE SINCE EEGA BEEVA CAN JUST TELL US WHERE THEY ARE!
THE DUCK AVENGER IS RIGHT...I GUESS EVEN A BLIND DUCK FINDS WATER EVERY ONCE AND A WHILE.

THAT'S A GOOD IDEA...IN THEORY. BUT I DON'T REMEMBER THE LOCATIONS!

!

?!

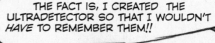

THE FACT IS, I CREATED THE ULTRADETECTOR SO THAT I WOULDN'T *HAVE* TO REMEMBER THEM!!

LOGICAL.

MAKES SENSE. HYUK!

IN ANY CASE, THE ULTRA-DETECTOR IS PROGRAMMED TO ONLY REVEAL THE ULTRAPODS' COORDINATES ONE AT A TIME! EMIL EAGLE AND HIS SINISTER 7 WERE ALREADY ABLE TO LOCATE THE FIRST ONE...

...IN SCROOGE MCDUCK'S MONEY BIN...

RIGHT!

...AFTER TELEPORTING IT TO AN *UNKNOWN LOCATION!*

SO *THAT'S* WHAT HAPPENED TO SCROOGE AND HIS MONEY BIN!

WE MUST PREVENT THE SINISTER 7 FROM GETTING THE ULTRAPODS AND CONSTRUCTING THE ULTRAMACHINE. FAILING TO DO SO WILL PUT THE ENTIRE WORLD IN TERRIBLE DANGER! SO...ARE YOU WITH US?

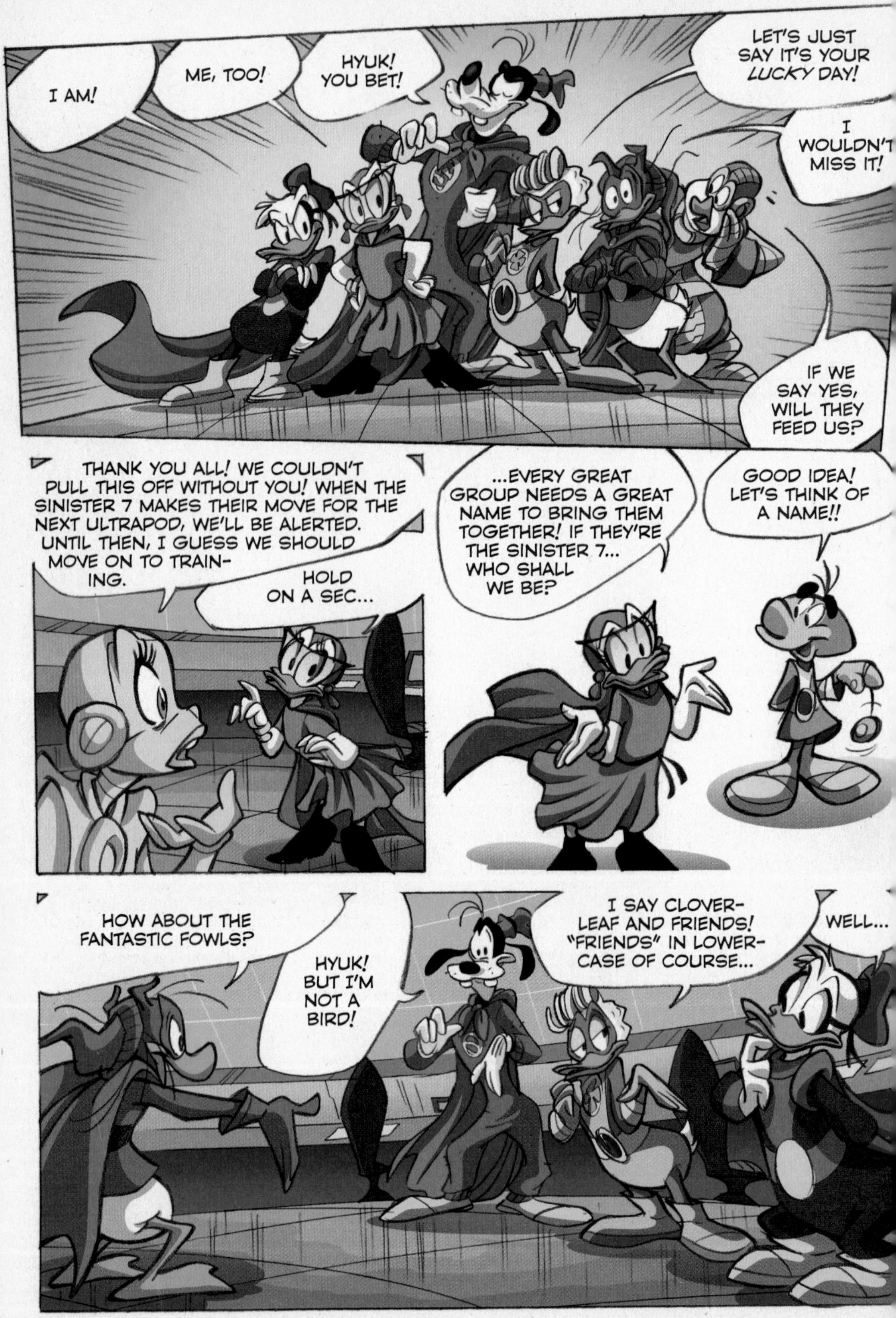
I AM!
ME, TOO!
HYUK! YOU BET!
LET'S JUST SAY IT'S YOUR LUCKY DAY!
I WOULDN'T MISS IT!
IF WE SAY YES, WILL THEY FEED US?
THANK YOU ALL! WE COULDN'T PULL THIS OFF WITHOUT YOU! WHEN THE SINISTER 7 MAKES THEIR MOVE FOR THE NEXT ULTRAPOD, WE'LL BE ALERTED. UNTIL THEN, I GUESS WE SHOULD MOVE ON TO TRAIN-ING.
HOLD ON A SEC...
...EVERY GREAT GROUP NEEDS A GREAT NAME TO BRING THEM TOGETHER! IF THEY'RE THE SINISTER 7... WHO SHALL WE BE?
GOOD IDEA! LET'S THINK OF A NAME!!
HOW ABOUT THE FANTASTIC FOWLS?
HYUK! BUT I'M NOT A BIRD!
I SAY CLOVER-LEAF AND FRIENDS! "FRIENDS" IN LOWER-CASE OF COURSE...
WELL...

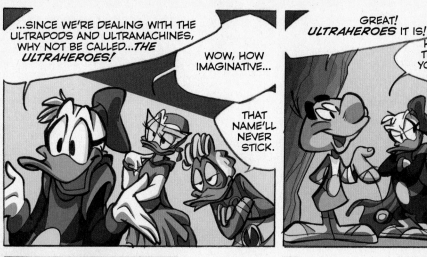

...SINCE WE'RE DEALING WITH THE ULTRAPODS AND ULTRAMACHINES, WHY NOT BE CALLED...*THE ULTRAHEROES!*

WOW, HOW IMAGINATIVE...

THAT NAME'LL NEVER STICK.

GREAT! *ULTRAHEROES* IT IS!

HA! HOW'S THAT TICKLE YOUR BEAK?!

)HMPF!(

YOU'VE ALL RECEIVED A BRAND NEW *ULTRA-SUIT!* PLEASE PUT THEM ON NOW, IF YOU HAVEN'T ALREADY.

YOU CAN ALL CHANGE IN YOUR ROOMS!

COME ON, GUYS!

PERHAPS A QUICK NAP BEFORE DINNER WOULD BE IN ORDER!

ROOMS

SORRY FOR THE CRAMPED QUARTERS, SCROOGE!

LET ME OUT OF HERE!

BACK TO UNCLE SCROOGE AND THE BOYS...

FORGET HIM! LET US OUT OF HERE!

LET YOU GO???

BUT IF I EVER DO WANT SOMEONE TO BUNGLE EVEN THE SIMPLEST OF JOBS, I'LL KNOW EXACTLY WHERE TO LOOK!

DANG! THAT WAS DOWNRIGHT HURTFUL...

BLESS ME BAGPIPES! THE ONLY THING TERRIBLE ABOUT YOU THREE IS HOW INCOMPETENT YOU ARE!

UM, EEGA BEEVA, IS THERE ANYTHING I CAN DO TO HELP?

LIKE WHAT?

I DON'T KNOW, BUT THERE MUST BE SOMETHING I CAN BE GOOD FOR...

UHHH MAYBE. I'LL LET YOU KNOW.

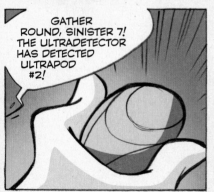

GATHER ROUND, SINISTER 7! THE ULTRADETECTOR HAS DETECTED ULTRAPOD #2!

IT'S LOCATED AT DUCKBURG STADIUM! THERE'S CURRENTLY A GAME GOING ON THERE...WHICH SHOULD MAKE THIS EVEN MORE FUN!

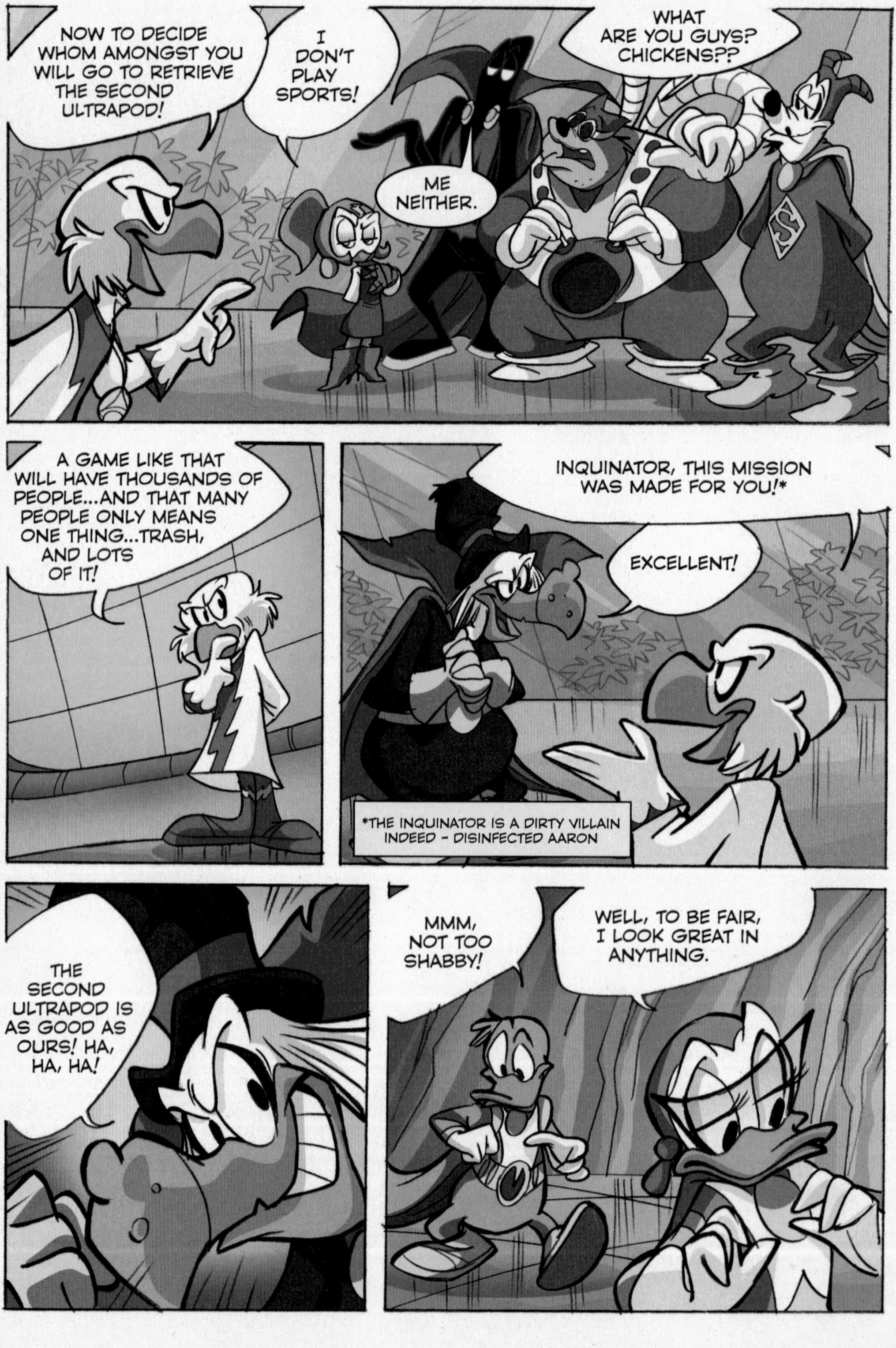

NOW TO DECIDE WHOM AMONGST YOU WILL GO TO RETRIEVE THE SECOND ULTRAPOD!
I DON'T PLAY SPORTS!
WHAT ARE YOU GUYS? CHICKENS??
ME NEITHER.
A GAME LIKE THAT WILL HAVE THOUSANDS OF PEOPLE...AND THAT MANY PEOPLE ONLY MEANS ONE THING...TRASH, AND LOTS OF IT!
INQUINATOR, THIS MISSION WAS MADE FOR YOU!*
EXCELLENT!
*THE INQUINATOR IS A DIRTY VILLAIN INDEED - DISINFECTED AARON
THE SECOND ULTRAPOD IS AS GOOD AS OURS! HA, HA, HA!
MMM, NOT TOO SHABBY!
WELL, TO BE FAIR, I LOOK GREAT IN ANYTHING.

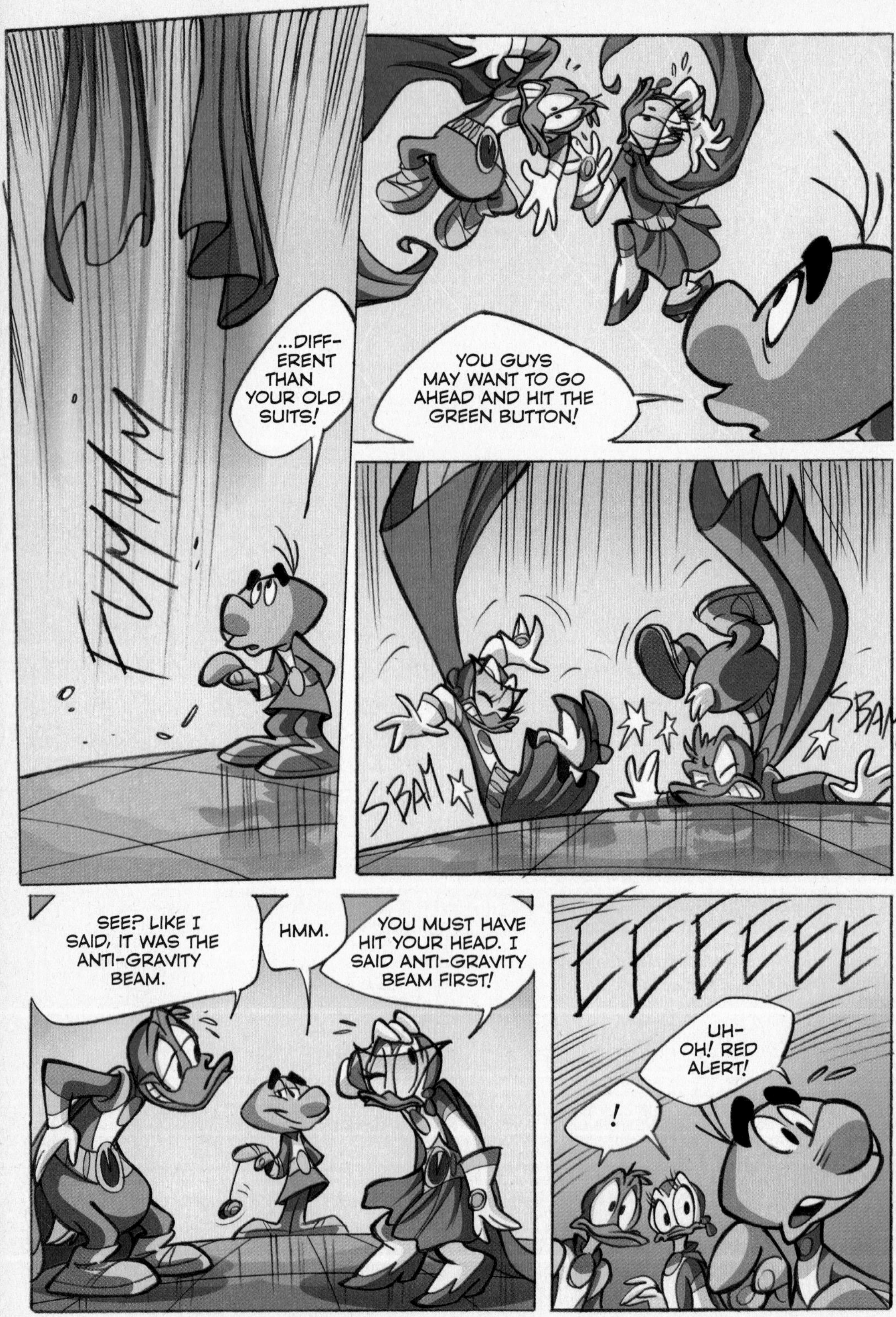
FUMMM
...DIFF-ERENT THAN YOUR OLD SUITS!
YOU GUYS MAY WANT TO GO AHEAD AND HIT THE GREEN BUTTON!
SBAM
SBAM
SEE? LIKE I SAID, IT WAS THE ANTI-GRAVITY BEAM.
HMM.
YOU MUST HAVE HIT YOUR HEAD. I SAID ANTI-GRAVITY BEAM FIRST!
EEEEEE
UH-OH! RED ALERT!
!

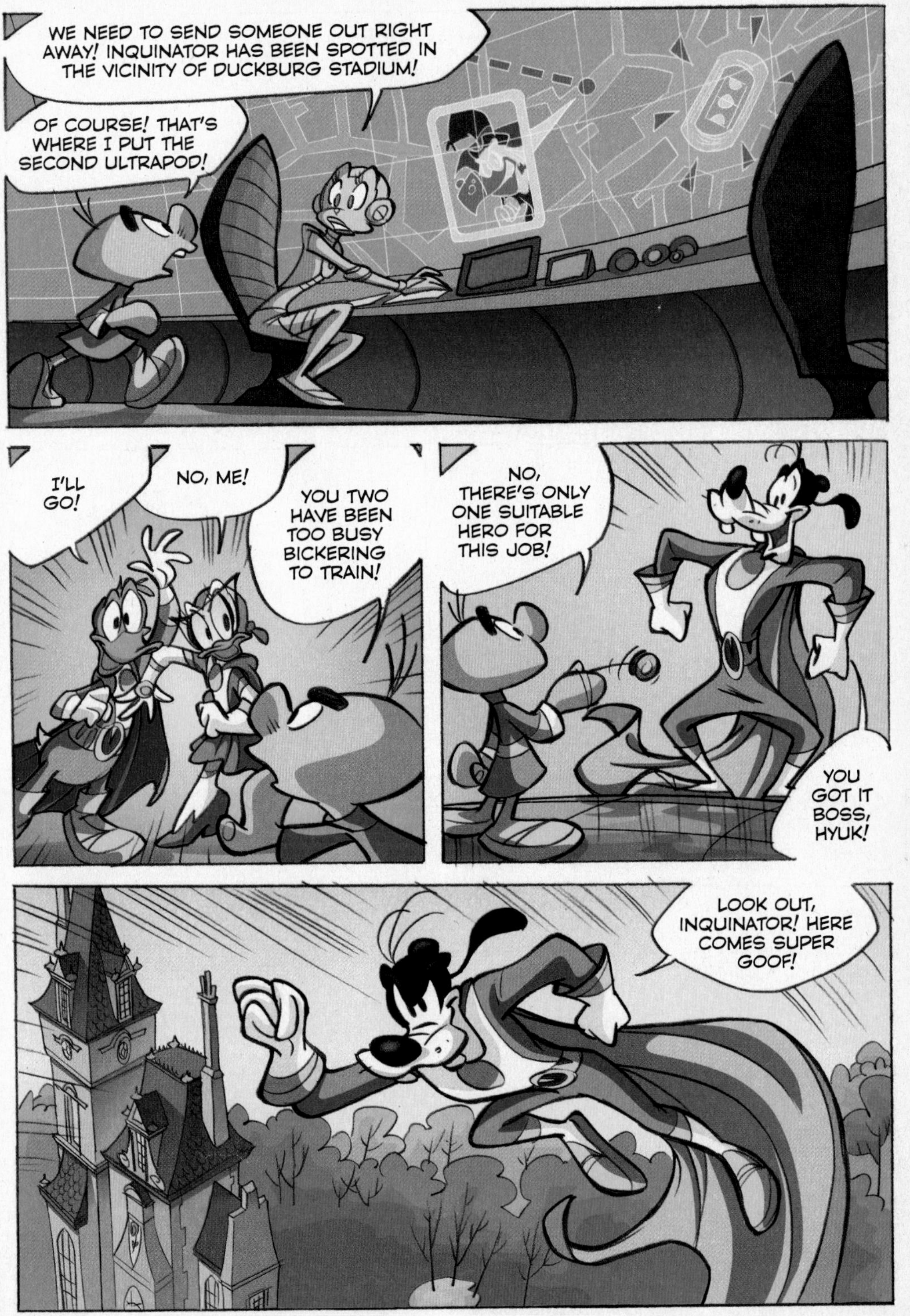
WE NEED TO SEND SOMEONE OUT RIGHT AWAY! INQUINATOR HAS BEEN SPOTTED IN THE VICINITY OF DUCKBURG STADIUM!
OF COURSE! THAT'S WHERE I PUT THE SECOND ULTRAPOD!
I'LL GO!
NO, ME!
YOU TWO HAVE BEEN TOO BUSY BICKERING TO TRAIN!
NO, THERE'S ONLY ONE SUITABLE HERO FOR THIS JOB!
YOU GOT IT BOSS, HYUK!
LOOK OUT, INQUINATOR! HERE COMES SUPER GOOF!

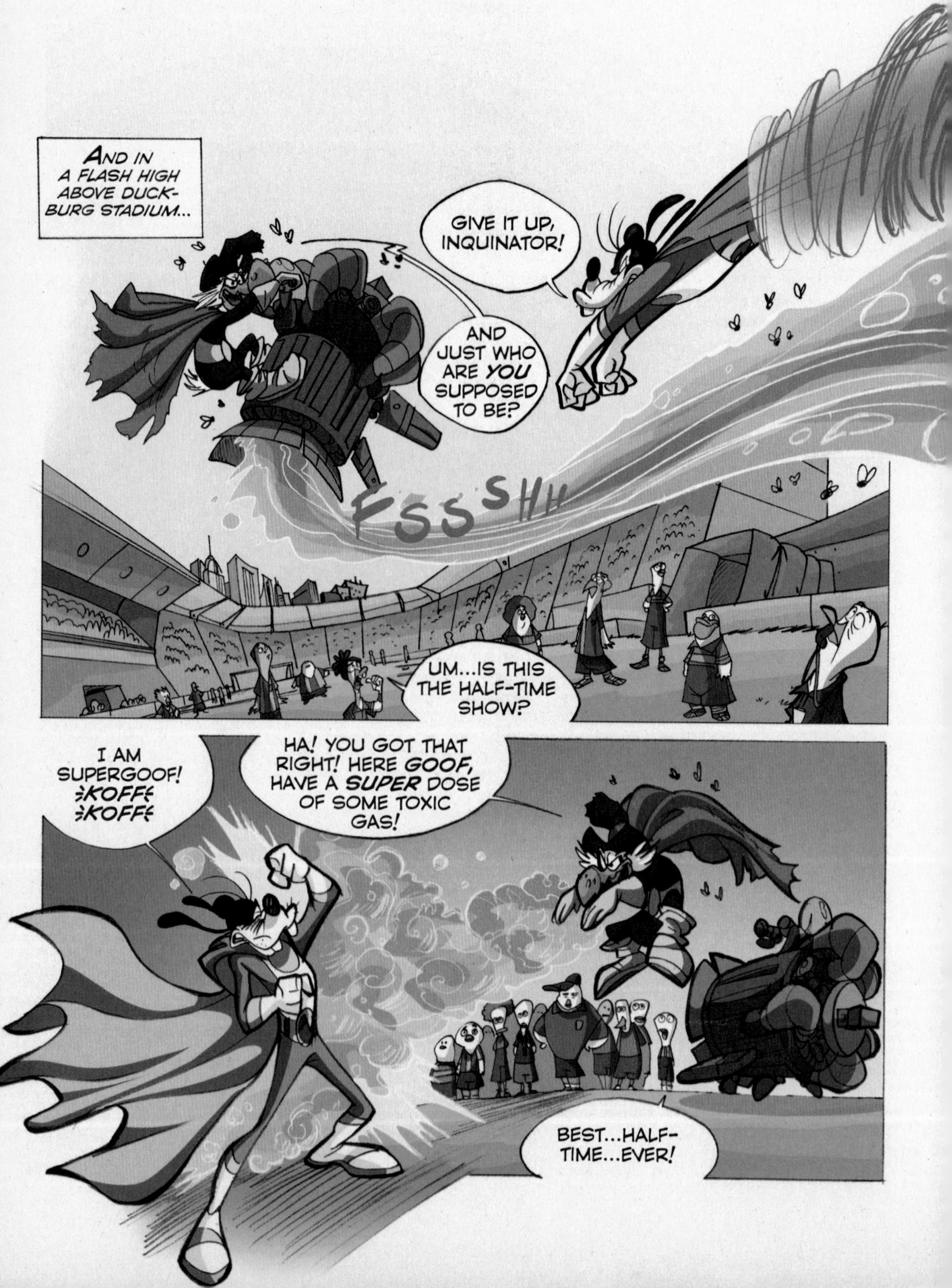
AND IN A FLASH HIGH ABOVE DUCK-BURG STADIUM...
GIVE IT UP, INQUINATOR!
AND JUST WHO ARE YOU SUPPOSED TO BE?
FSSSHH
UM...IS THIS THE HALF-TIME SHOW?
I AM SUPERGOOF! KOFF KOFF
HA! YOU GOT THAT RIGHT! HERE GOOF, HAVE A SUPER DOSE OF SOME TOXIC GAS!
BEST...HALF-TIME...EVER!

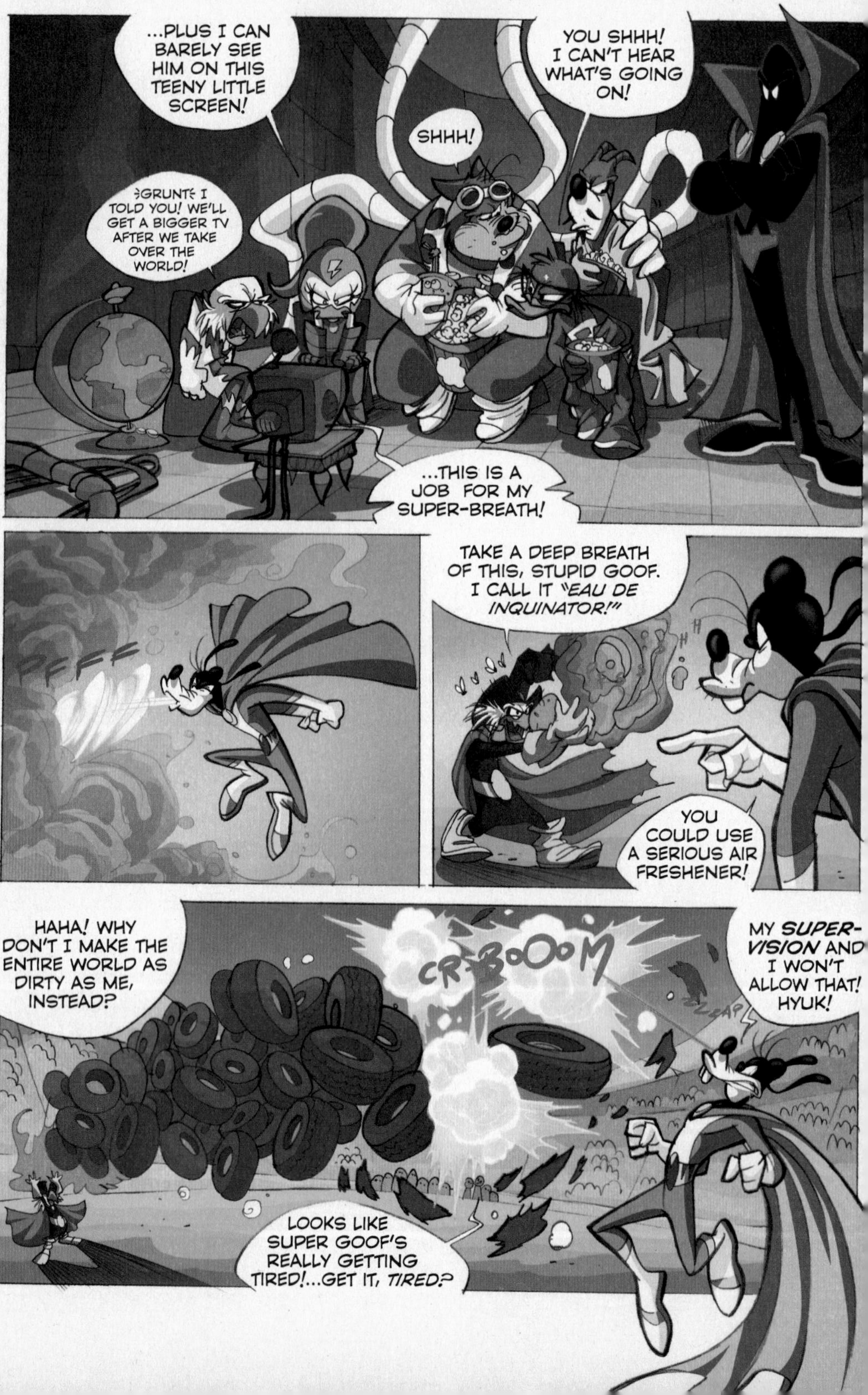
...PLUS I CAN BARELY SEE HIM ON THIS TEENY LITTLE SCREEN!
SHHH!
YOU SHHH! I CAN'T HEAR WHAT'S GOING ON!
GRUNT I TOLD YOU! WE'LL GET A BIGGER TV AFTER WE TAKE OVER THE WORLD!
...THIS IS A JOB FOR MY SUPER-BREATH!
PFFFF
TAKE A DEEP BREATH OF THIS, STUPID GOOF. I CALL IT "EAU DE INQUINATOR!"
YOU COULD USE A SERIOUS AIR FRESHENER!
HAHA! WHY DON'T I MAKE THE ENTIRE WORLD AS DIRTY AS ME, INSTEAD?
CR-BOOOM
MY SUPER-VISION AND I WON'T ALLOW THAT! HYUK!
LOOKS LIKE SUPER GOOF'S REALLY GETTING TIRED!...GET IT, TIRED?

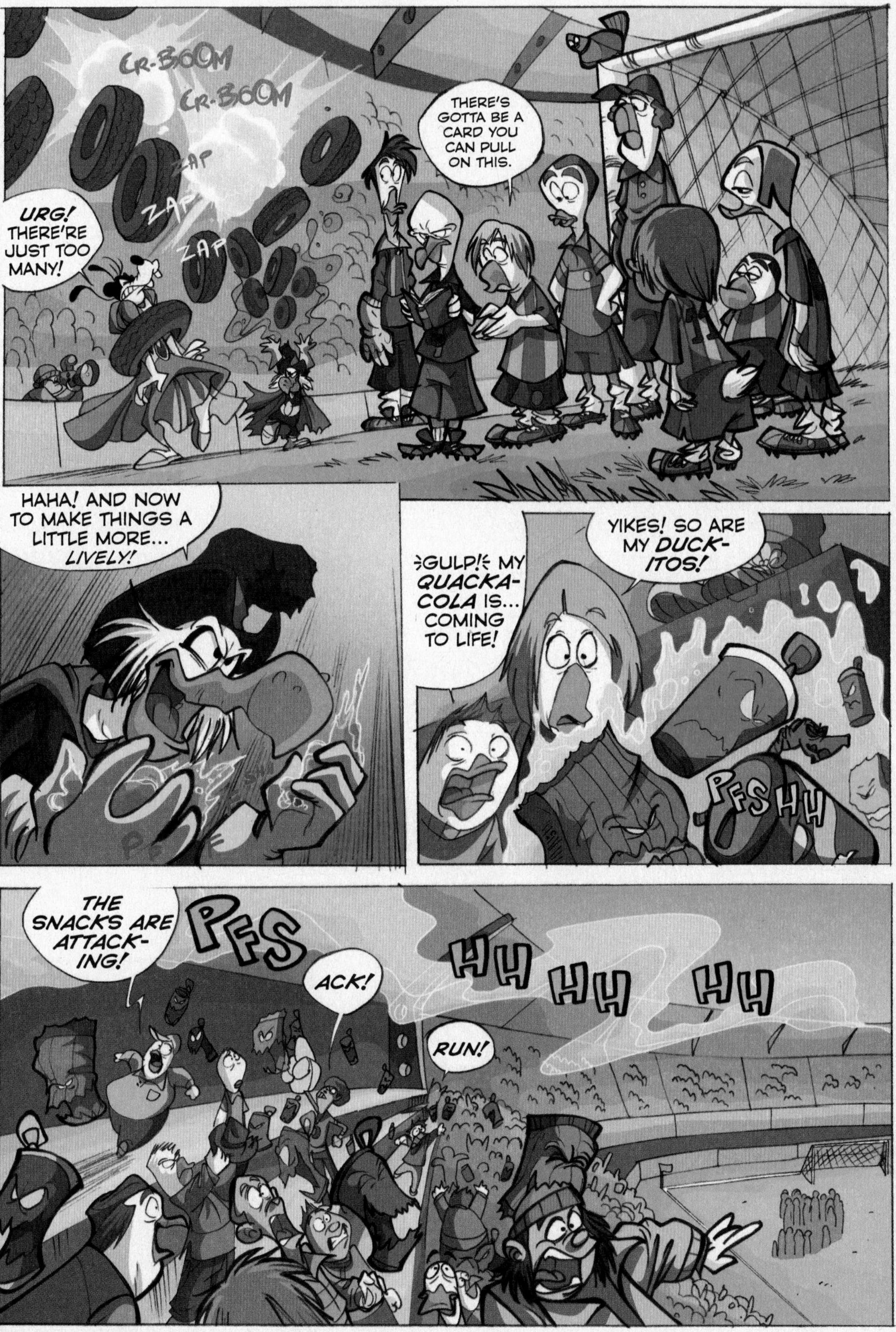
CR-BOOM
CR-BOOM
ZAP
ZAP
ZAP
URG! THERE'RE JUST TOO MANY!
THERE'S GOTTA BE A CARD YOU CAN PULL ON THIS.
HAHA! AND NOW TO MAKE THINGS A LITTLE MORE... LIVELY!
GULP! MY QUACKA-COLA IS... COMING TO LIFE!
YIKES! SO ARE MY DUCK-ITOS!
PFSHH
THE SNACKS ARE ATTACK-ING!
PFS
ACK!
HH HH HH
RUN!

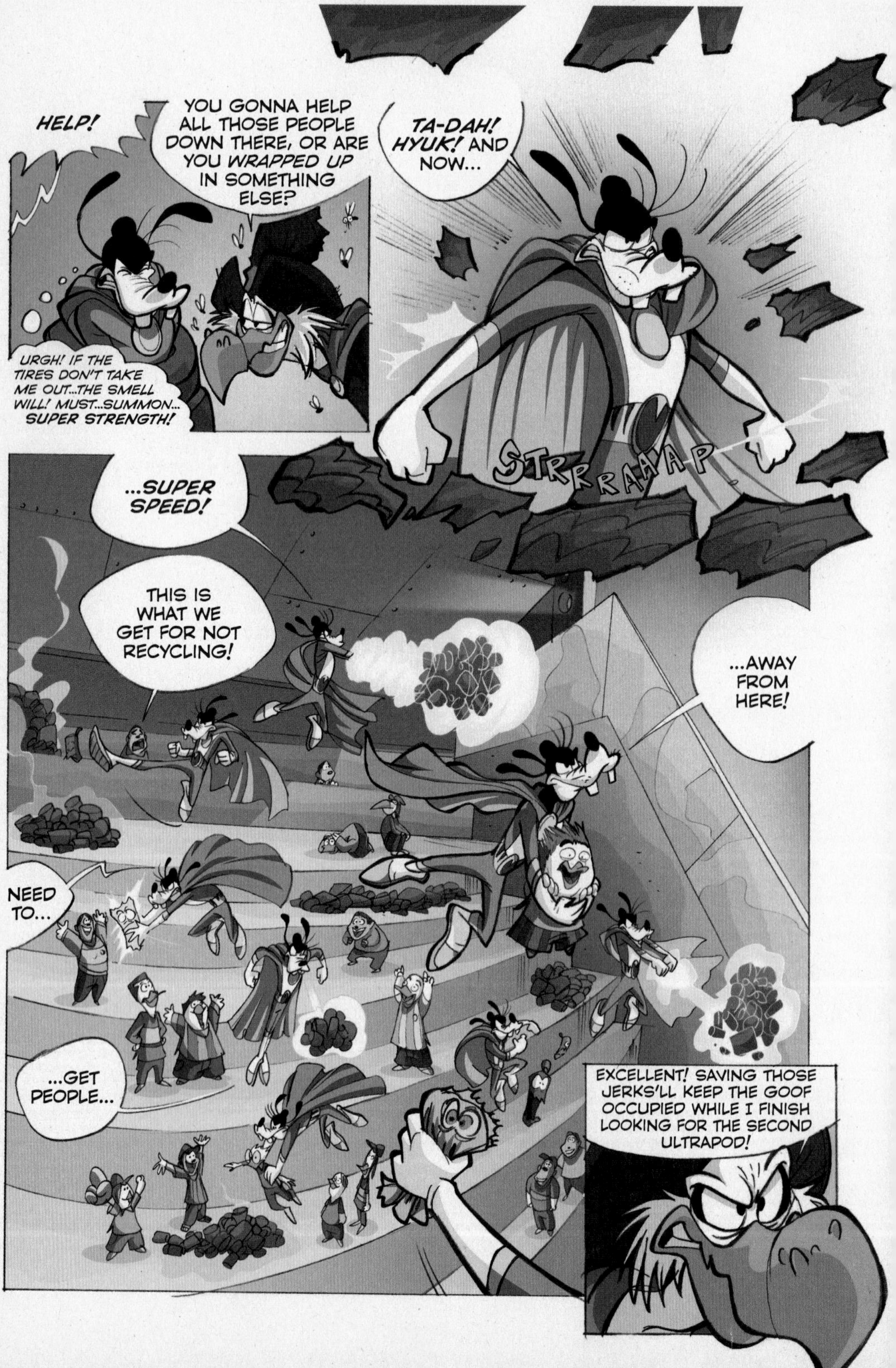
HELP!
YOU GONNA HELP ALL THOSE PEOPLE DOWN THERE, OR ARE YOU WRAPPED UP IN SOMETHING ELSE?
URGH! IF THE TIRES DON'T TAKE ME OUT...THE SMELL WILL! MUST...SUMMON... SUPER STRENGTH!
TA-DAH! HYUK! AND NOW...
STRRRAAAAP
...SUPER SPEED!
THIS IS WHAT WE GET FOR NOT RECYCLING!
...AWAY FROM HERE!
NEED TO...
...GET PEOPLE...
EXCELLENT! SAVING THOSE JERKS'LL KEEP THE GOOF OCCUPIED WHILE I FINISH LOOKING FOR THE SECOND ULTRAPOD!

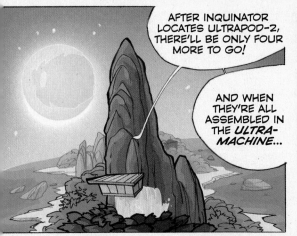

AFTER INQUINATOR LOCATES ULTRAPOD-2, THERE'LL BE ONLY FOUR MORE TO GO!

AND WHEN THEY'RE ALL ASSEMBLED IN THE *ULTRA-MACHINE*...

...THE WORLD...

...WILL BE *OURS!*

MEANING, *MINE!*

AKA, *MINE!*

MINE!

NO, *MINE!*

MINE, ALL *MINE!*

OF COURSE I MEAN *MINE!* HEH, HEH!

BUT, FIRST...

...WE NEED TO FIGURE OUT WHERE THAT *SUPER GOOF* CAME FROM!

SOMEONE HAD TO HAVE SENT HIM TO THE STADIUM! SOMEONE WHO KNOWS ABOUT THE ULTRAMACHINE! AND I THINK I KNOW JUST *WHO* THAT SOMEONE *IS...*

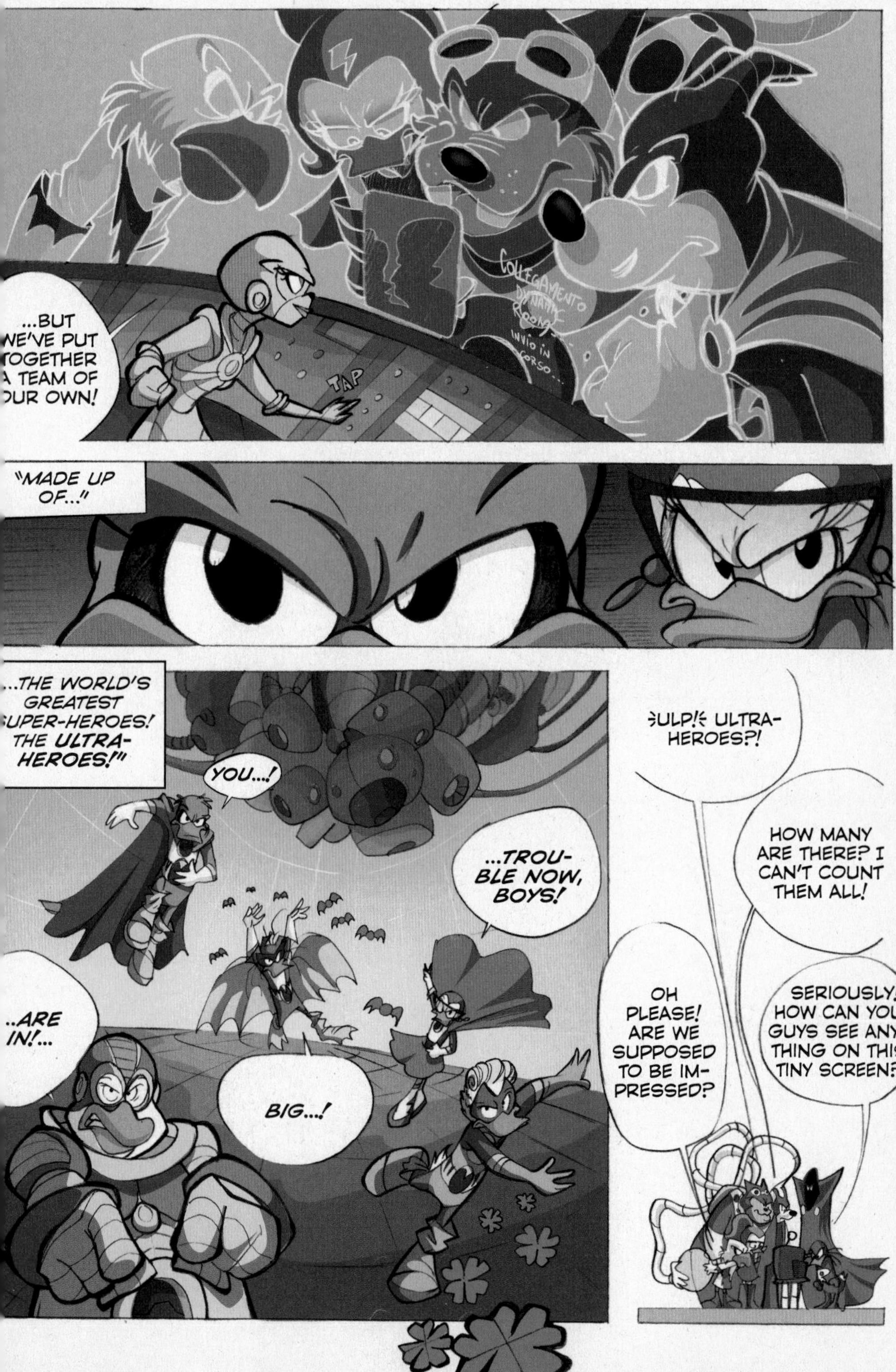
...BUT WE'VE PUT TOGETHER A TEAM OF OUR OWN!
TAP
COLLEGAMENTO DYNAMIC ROOMS INVIO IN CORSO...
"MADE UP OF..."
...THE WORLD'S GREATEST SUPER-HEROES! THE ULTRA-HEROES!"
YOU...!
...TROUBLE NOW, BOYS!
..ARE IN!...
BIG...!
GULP! ULTRA-HEROES?!
HOW MANY ARE THERE? I CAN'T COUNT THEM ALL!
OH PLEASE! ARE WE SUPPOSED TO BE IMPRESSED?
SERIOUSLY! HOW CAN YOU GUYS SEE ANYTHING ON THIS TINY SCREEN?

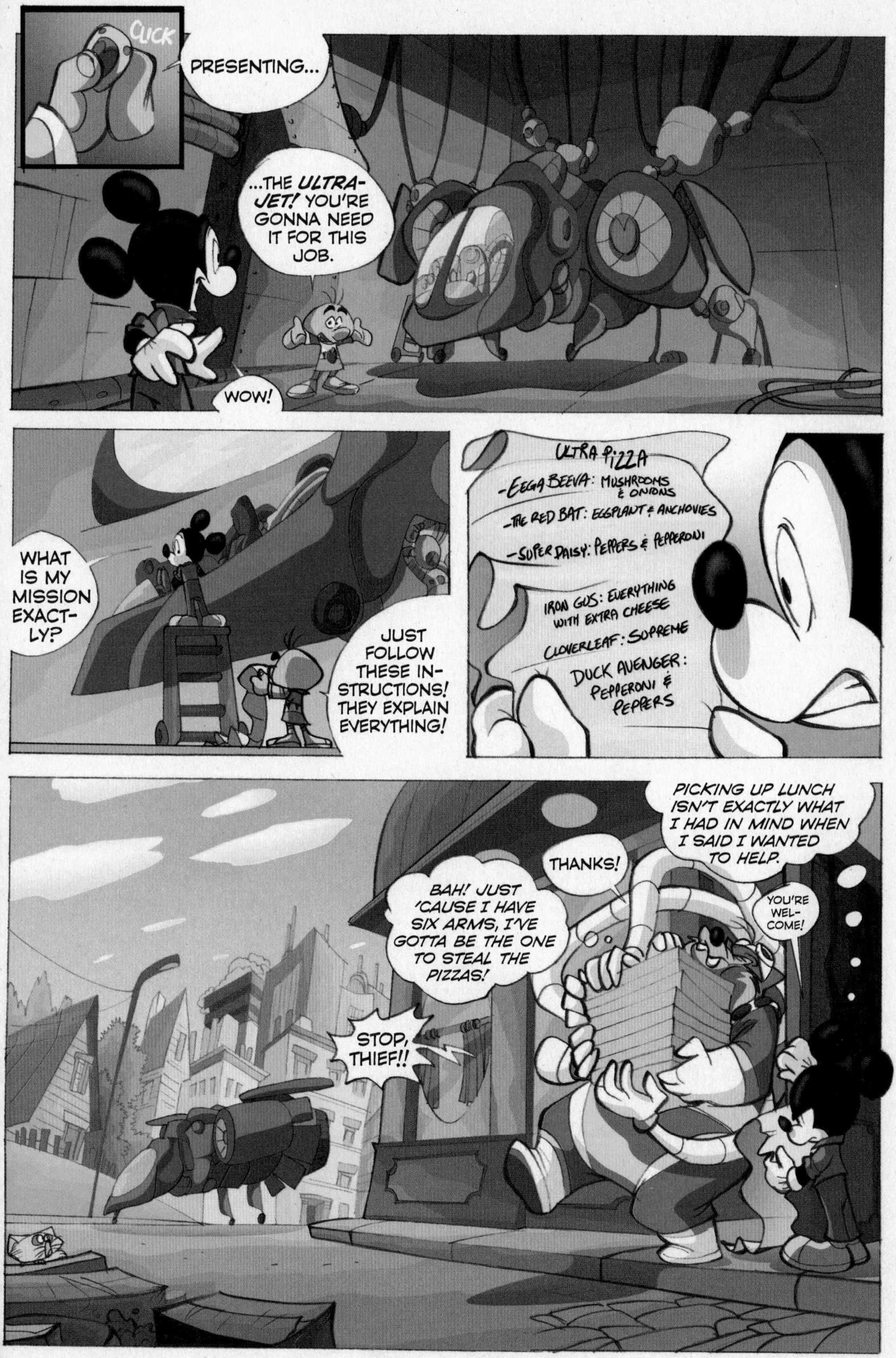
CLICK
PRESENTING...
...THE ULTRA-JET! YOU'RE GONNA NEED IT FOR THIS JOB.
WOW!
WHAT IS MY MISSION EXACT-LY?
JUST FOLLOW THESE IN-STRUCTIONS! THEY EXPLAIN EVERYTHING!
ULTRA PIZZA
-EEGA BEEVA: MUSHROOMS & ONIONS
-THE RED BAT: EGGPLANT & ANCHOVIES
-SUPER DAISY: PEPPERS & PEPPERONI
IRON GUS: EVERYTHING WITH EXTRA CHEESE
CLOVERLEAF: SUPREME
DUCK AVENGER: PEPPERONI & PEPPERS
PICKING UP LUNCH ISN'T EXACTLY WHAT I HAD IN MIND WHEN I SAID I WANTED TO HELP.
THANKS!
YOU'RE WEL-COME!
BAH! JUST 'CAUSE I HAVE SIX ARMS, I'VE GOTTA BE THE ONE TO STEAL THE PIZZAS!
STOP, THIEF!!

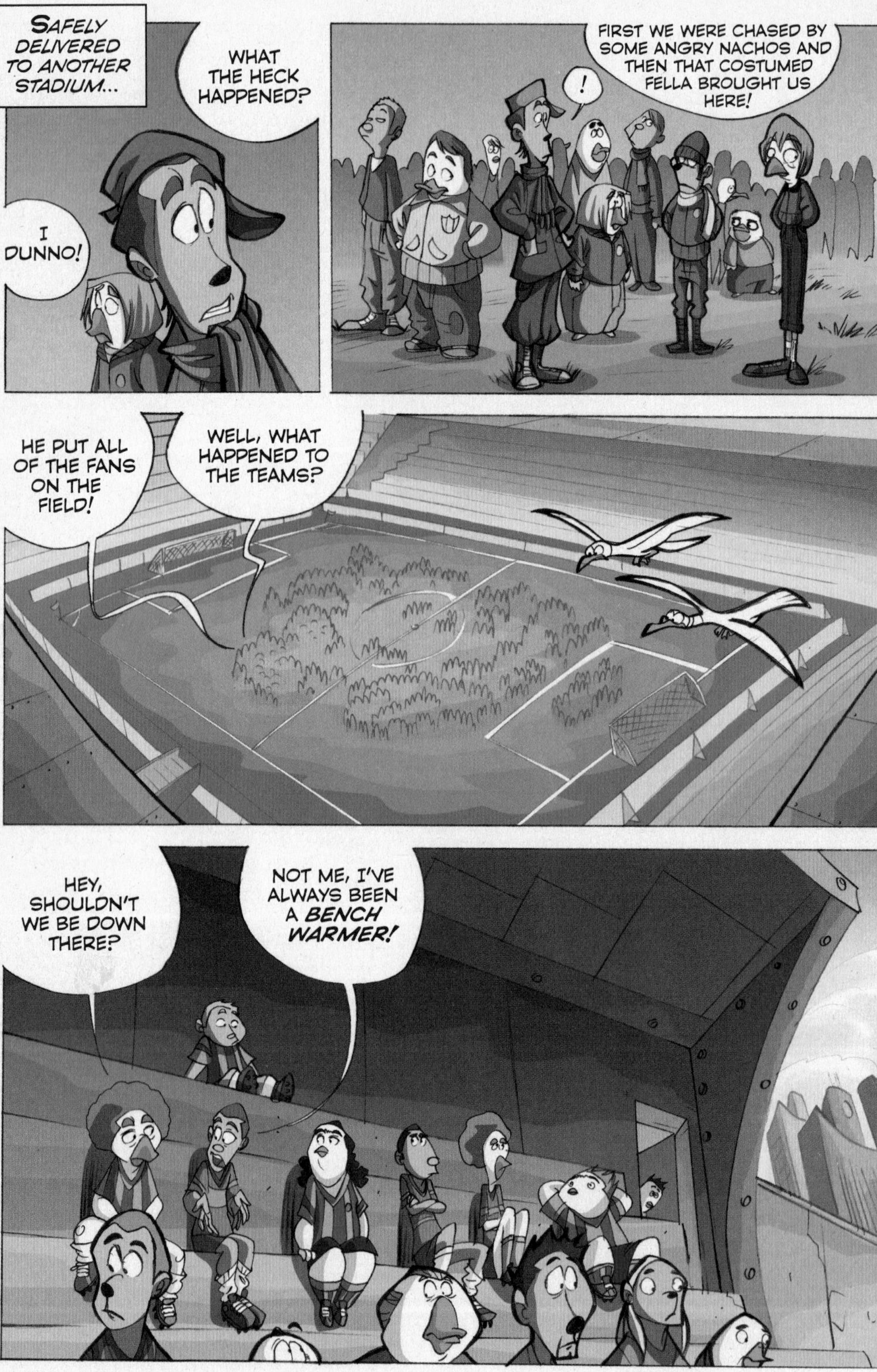
SAFELY DELIVERED TO ANOTHER STADIUM...
WHAT THE HECK HAPPENED?
I DUNNO!
FIRST WE WERE CHASED BY SOME ANGRY NACHOS AND THEN THAT COSTUMED FELLA BROUGHT US HERE!
!
HE PUT ALL OF THE FANS ON THE FIELD!
WELL, WHAT HAPPENED TO THE TEAMS?
HEY, SHOULDN'T WE BE DOWN THERE?
NOT ME, I'VE ALWAYS BEEN A BENCH WARMER!

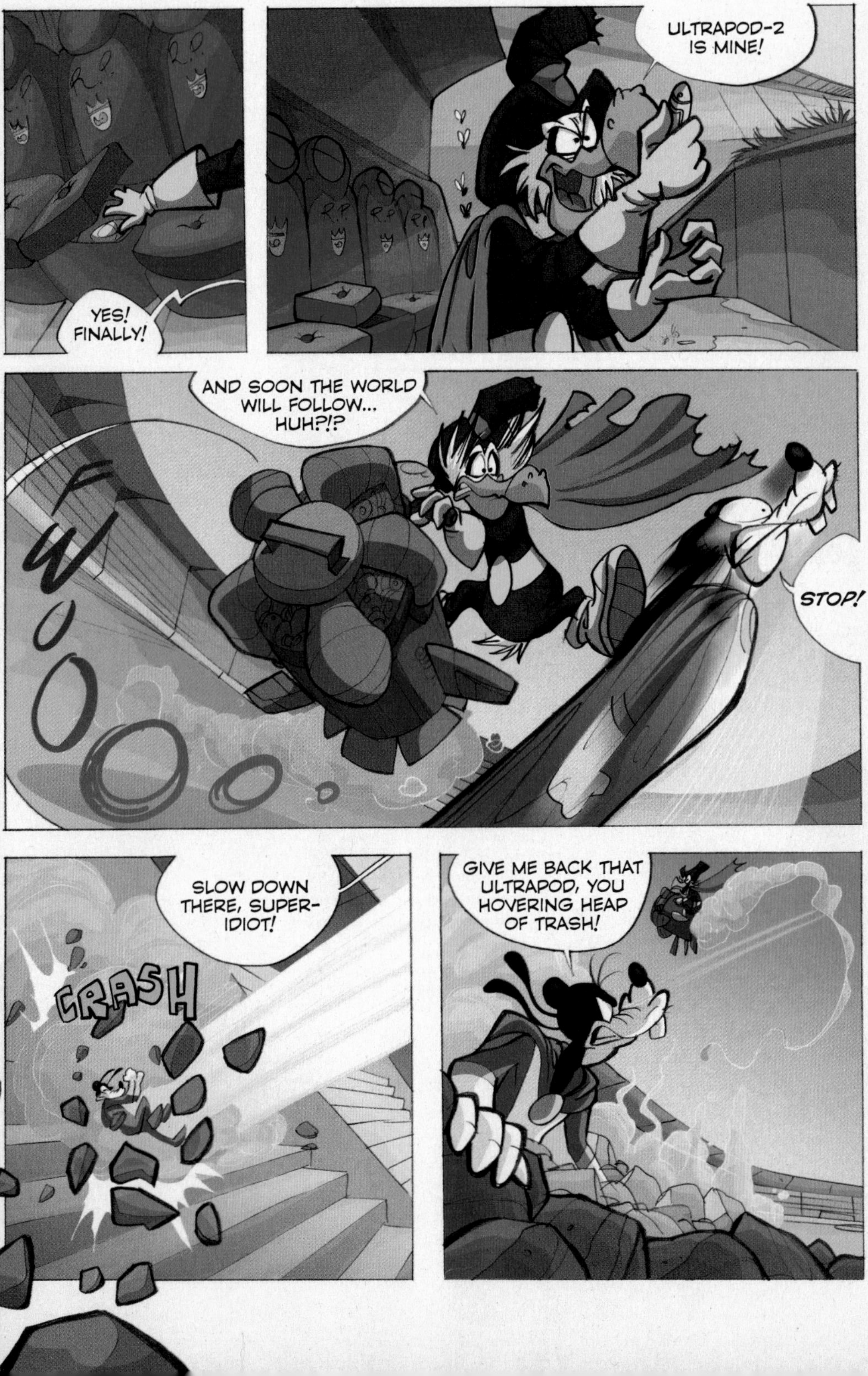
YES! FINALLY!
ULTRAPOD-2 IS MINE!
AND SOON THE WORLD WILL FOLLOW... HUH?!?
FWOOO
STOP!
SLOW DOWN THERE, SUPER-IDIOT!
CRASH
GIVE ME BACK THAT ULTRAPOD, YOU HOVERING HEAP OF TRASH!

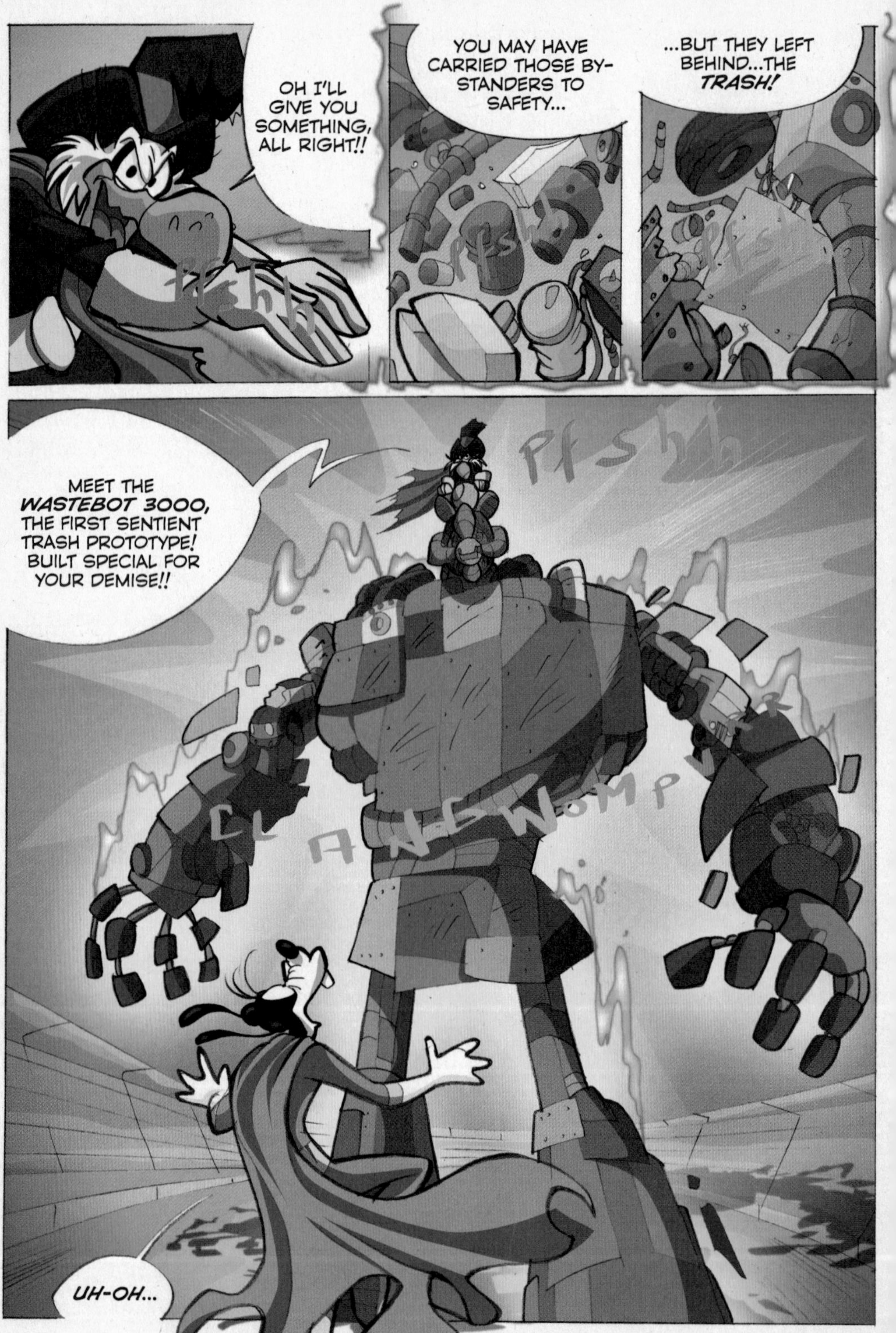
OH I'LL GIVE YOU SOMETHING, ALL RIGHT!!
Pfshh
YOU MAY HAVE CARRIED THOSE BY-STANDERS TO SAFETY...
...BUT THEY LEFT BEHIND...THE *TRASH!*
MEET THE *WASTEBOT 3000,* THE FIRST SENTIENT TRASH PROTOTYPE! BUILT SPECIAL FOR YOUR DEMISE!!
Pfshh
CLANGWOMP
UH-OH...

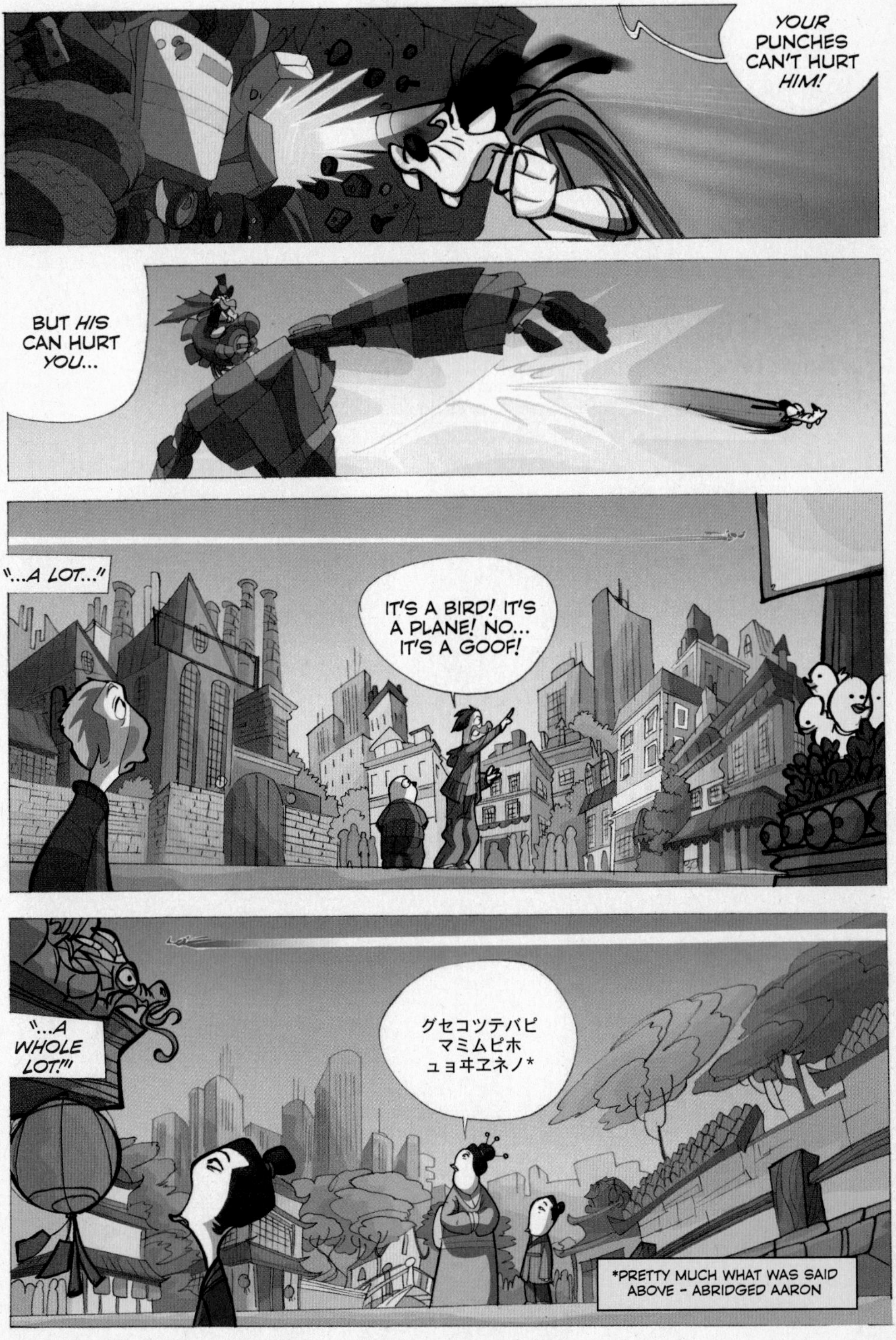
YOUR PUNCHES CAN'T HURT HIM!
BUT HIS CAN HURT YOU...
"...A LOT..."
IT'S A BIRD! IT'S A PLANE! NO... IT'S A GOOF!
"...A WHOLE LOT!"
グセコツテバピ
マミムピホ
ユヨヰヱネノ*
*PRETTY MUCH WHAT WAS SAID ABOVE - ABRIDGED AARON

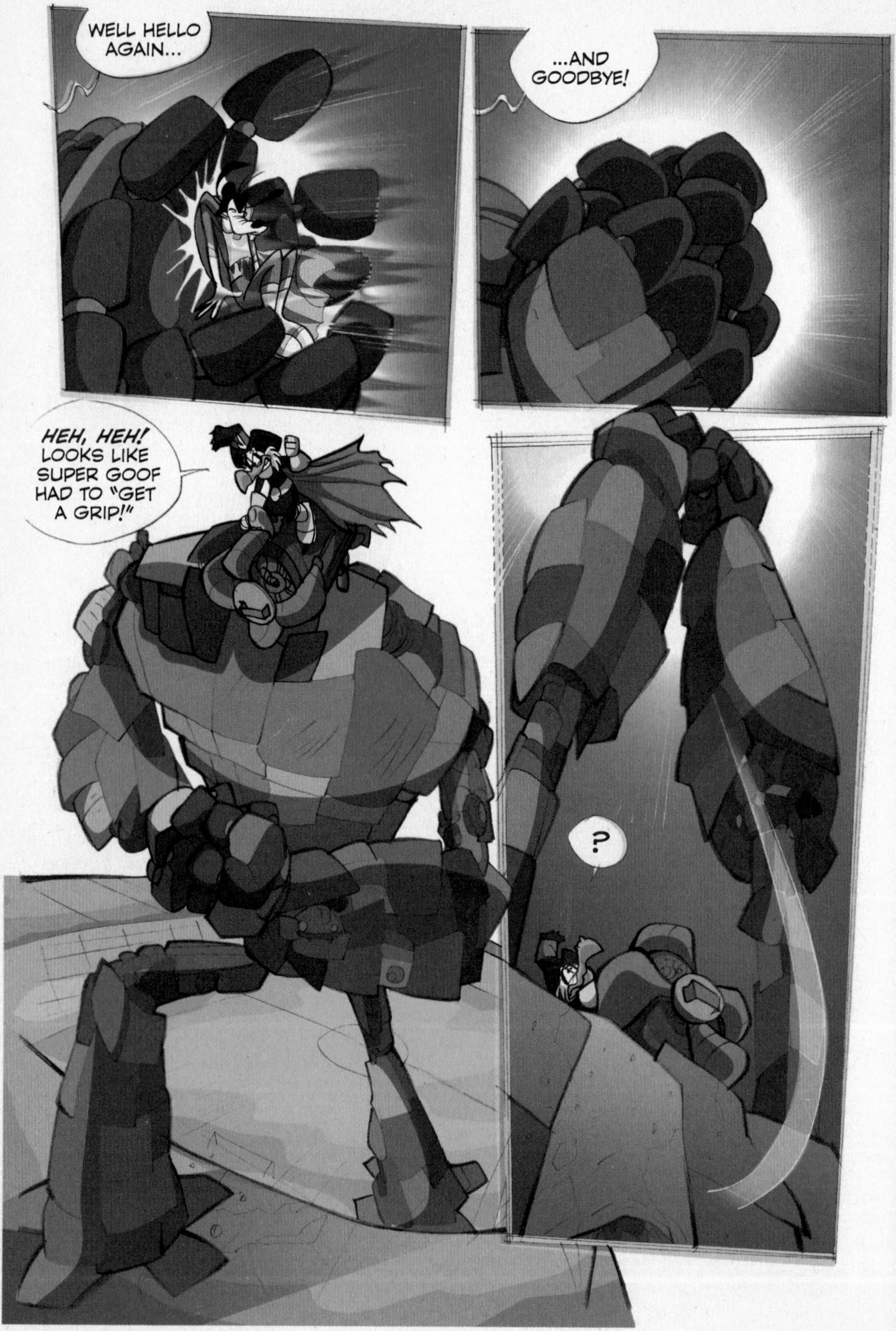
WELL HELLO AGAIN...
...AND GOODBYE!
HEH, HEH! LOOKS LIKE SUPER GOOF HAD TO "GET A GRIP!"
?

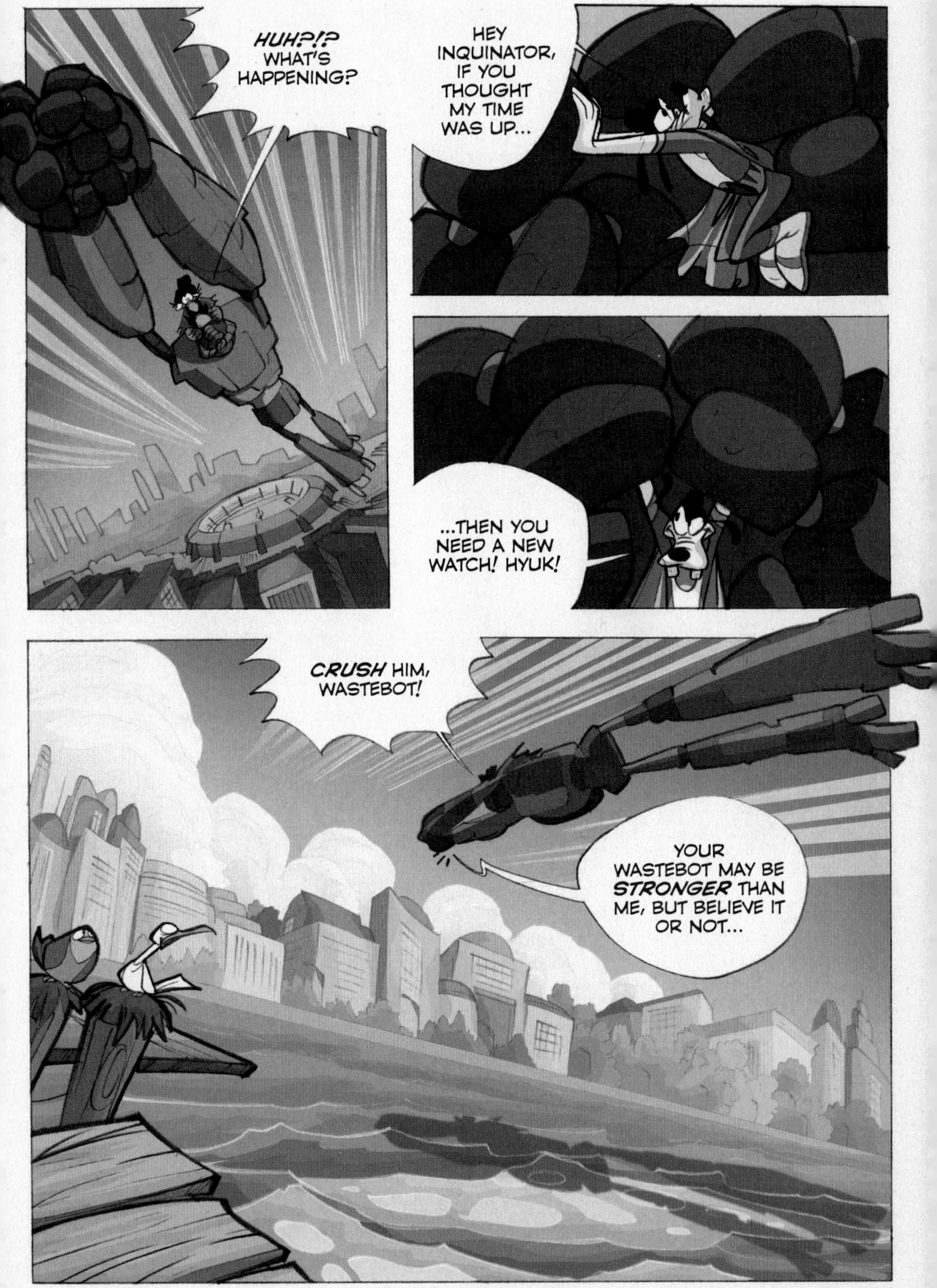
HUH?!? WHAT'S HAPPENING?
HEY INQUINATOR, IF YOU THOUGHT MY TIME WAS UP...
...THEN YOU NEED A NEW WATCH! HYUK!
CRUSH HIM, WASTEBOT!
YOUR WASTEBOT MAY BE STRONGER THAN ME, BUT BELIEVE IT OR NOT...

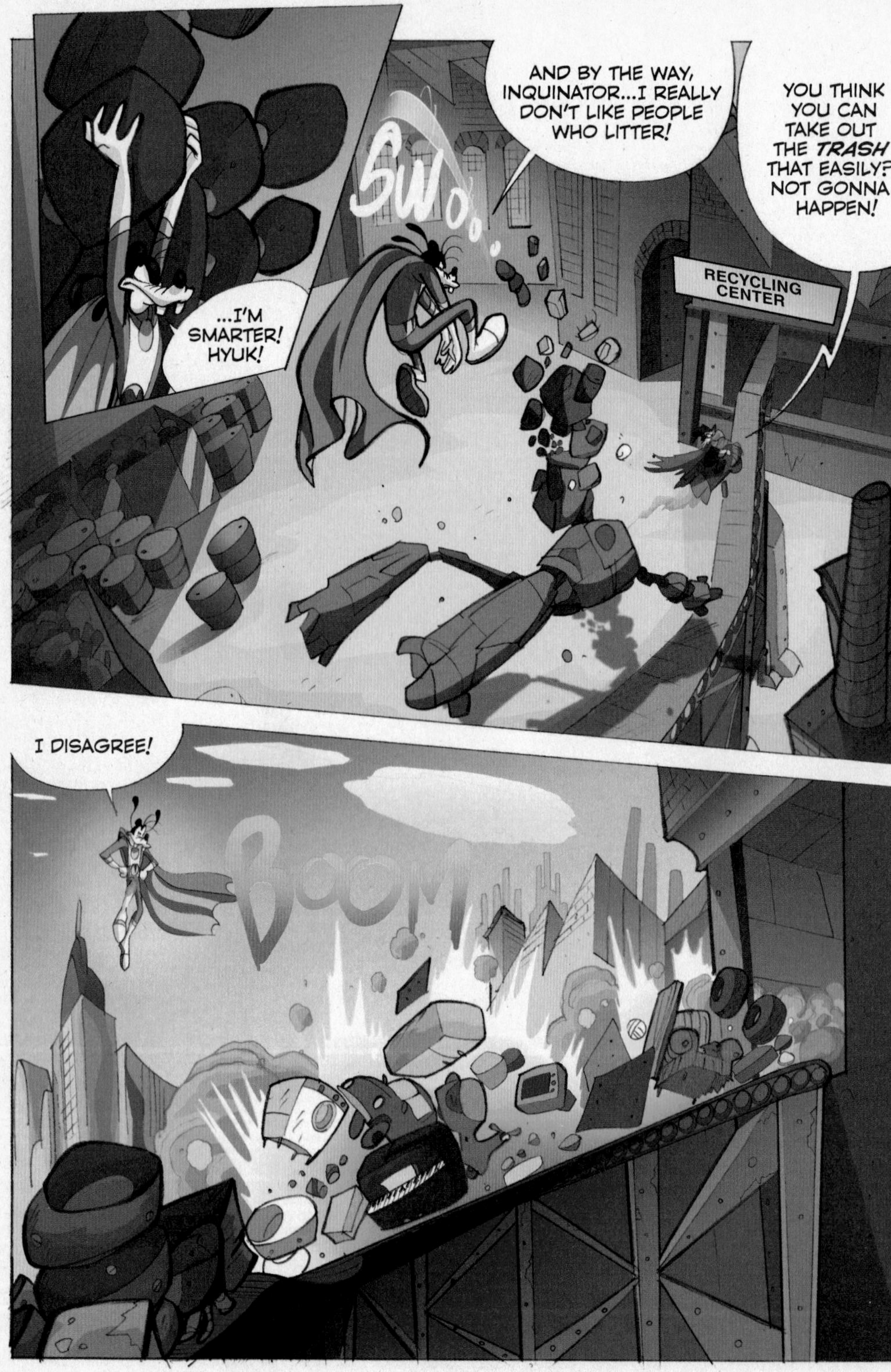
...I'M SMARTER! HYUK!
SWOO
AND BY THE WAY, INQUINATOR...I REALLY DON'T LIKE PEOPLE WHO LITTER!
YOU THINK YOU CAN TAKE OUT THE *TRASH* THAT EASILY? NOT GONNA HAPPEN!
RECYCLING CENTER
I DISAGREE!
BOOM

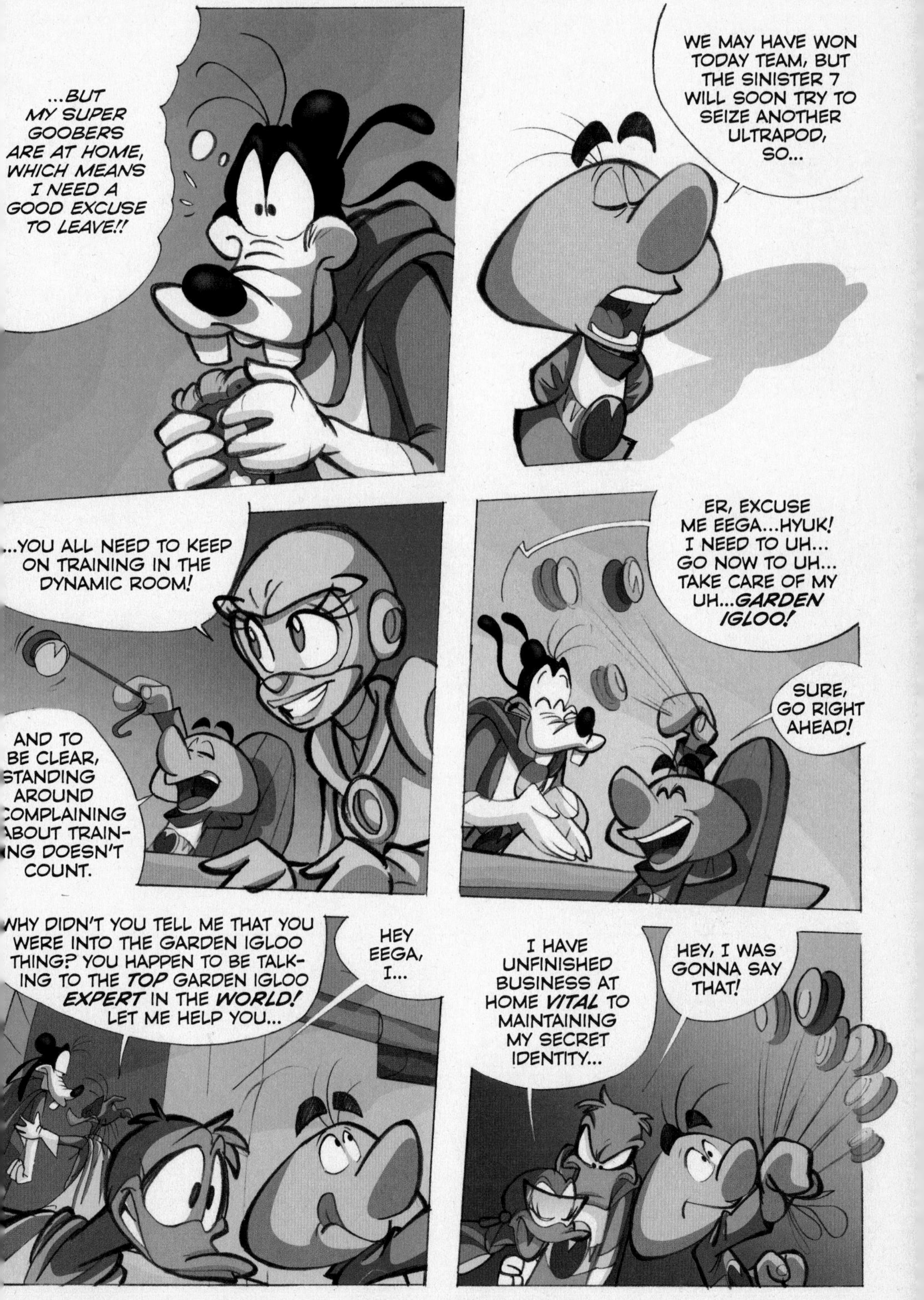
...BUT MY SUPER GOOBERS ARE AT HOME, WHICH MEANS I NEED A GOOD EXCUSE TO LEAVE!!
WE MAY HAVE WON TODAY TEAM, BUT THE SINISTER 7 WILL SOON TRY TO SEIZE ANOTHER ULTRAPOD, SO...
...YOU ALL NEED TO KEEP ON TRAINING IN THE DYNAMIC ROOM!
AND TO BE CLEAR, STANDING AROUND COMPLAINING ABOUT TRAINING DOESN'T COUNT.
ER, EXCUSE ME EEGA...HYUK! I NEED TO UH... GO NOW TO UH... TAKE CARE OF MY UH...GARDEN IGLOO!
SURE, GO RIGHT AHEAD!
WHY DIDN'T YOU TELL ME THAT YOU WERE INTO THE GARDEN IGLOO THING? YOU HAPPEN TO BE TALKING TO THE TOP GARDEN IGLOO EXPERT IN THE WORLD! LET ME HELP YOU...
HEY EEGA, I...
I HAVE UNFINISHED BUSINESS AT HOME VITAL TO MAINTAINING MY SECRET IDENTITY...
HEY, I WAS GONNA SAY THAT!

WELL IT'S NOT MY FAULT IF YOU SPEAK TOO SLOW!

OH GEEZ! HOW DOES YOUR *BOYFRIEND* PUT UP WITH YOU??

ENOUGH, YOU TWO! JUST GO ALREADY!

MICKEY?

LET ME GUESS. TIME TO CLEAN UP EVERYONE'S DINNER?

NOT EXACTLY...

WE NEED TO FIND OUT EXACTLY *WHERE* SCROOGE AND HIS MONEY BIN ENDED UP!

REALLY?

EMIL EAGLE IS PROBABLY HOLDING HIM CAPTIVE SOMEWHERE!

HERE IS A RECORDING FROM THE MONEY BIN'S CAMERAS...

I'M ON IT! YOU CAN COUNT ON ME!

OUR SATELLITE INTERCEPTED THE VIDEO, BUT THE *ORIGINAL COORDINATES* ARE ENCRYPTED...

GOOD LUCK, MICKEY. WE'RE DEPENDING ON YOU!

28:11:97

‡MUMBLE‡

SO FAR, THERE'S NOT A SINGLE CLUE!

I'LL RUN THE VIDEO ONE MORE TIME...

...is the first step towards...

...world domination! *Ha! Ha! Ha!*

...his fault! *Ha! Ha! Ha!*

28:11:98

28:11:99

28:13:99

EVERYTHING LOOKS TO BE NORMAL...

ZOOM 300%

...EVEN WHEN I ZOOM IN...

...EXCEPT THOSE STRANGE PLANTS! MY FIRST LEAD!

C'MON! WE'VE BUSTED OUT OF HIGHER SECURITY PRISONS THAN THIS!

MOVE ASIDE, SCROOGE. THE *PROFESSIONALS* ARE WORKING!

AND HOW ARE YOU GOING TO NEUTRALIZE THE LASER GRID, *PROFESSIONALS?*

ERM...WE COULD...

OR MAYBE...

HMM... HAVE YOU GOT ANY IDEAS, SCROOGE?

DOPES!

BECAUSE OF YOU, WE LOST ULTRA-POD-2!

⇒GROAN⇐

HOW COULD YOU LET THAT IDIOT SUPER GOOF BEAT YOU!

GET OUT OF MY SIGHT!

⇒SIGH⇐

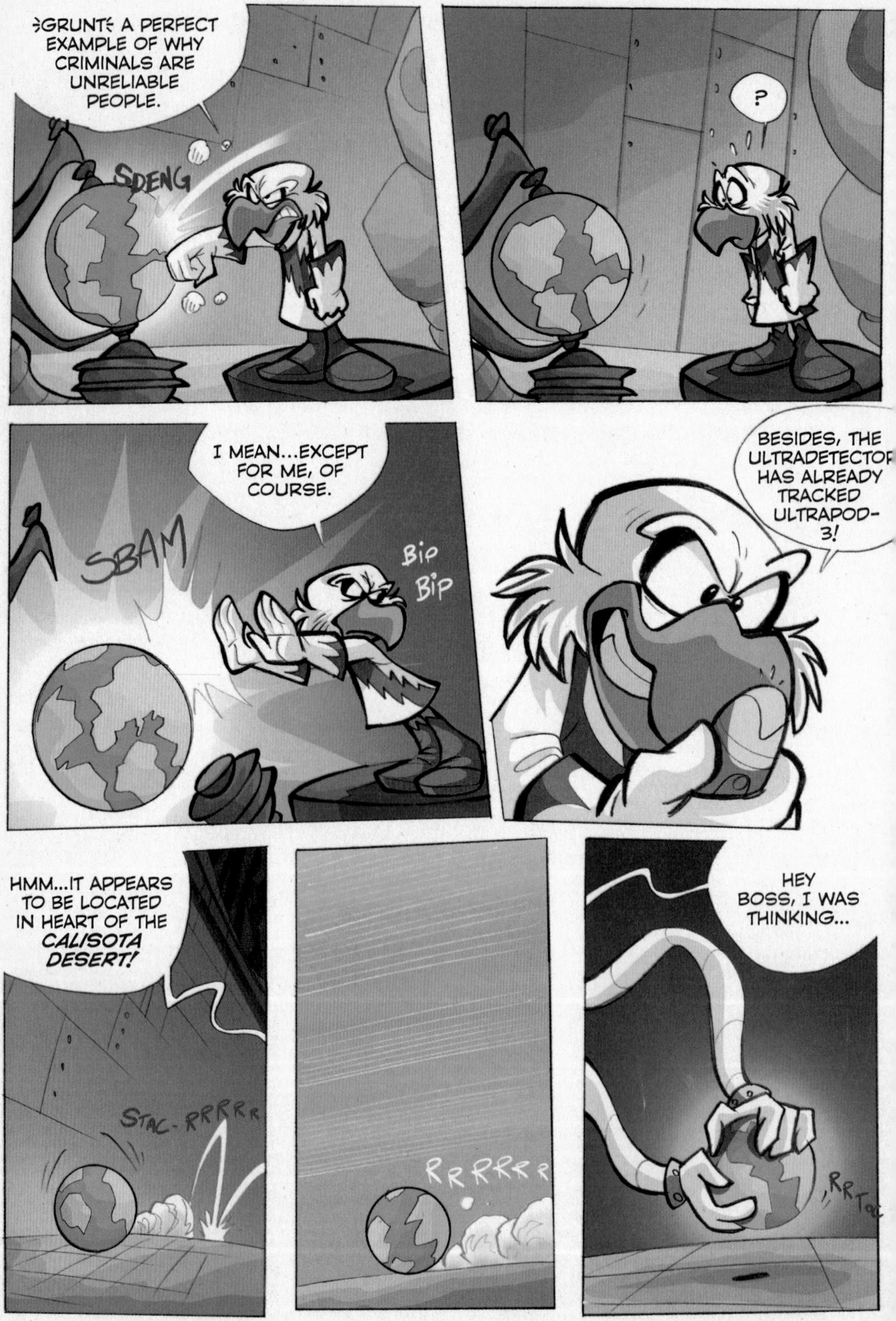

⋛GRUNT⋚ A PERFECT EXAMPLE OF WHY CRIMINALS ARE UNRELIABLE PEOPLE.
SDENG
?
I MEAN...EXCEPT FOR ME, OF COURSE.
SBAM
BIP BIP
BESIDES, THE ULTRADETECTOR HAS ALREADY TRACKED ULTRAPOD-3!
HMM...IT APPEARS TO BE LOCATED IN HEART OF THE *CALISOTA DESERT!*
STAC-RRRRRR
RRRRRR
HEY BOSS, I WAS THINKING...
RRTOC

...PEG-LEG PETE STILL HAS SOME TRICKS UP HIS SLEEVES!

AND PRESTO... WE'RE FREE!

DEFLECTING THE LASER GRID WITH SHINY COINS! I COULD'VE THOUGHT OF THAT.

BZZZ

I HIGHLY DOUBT IT. AND YOU CERTAINLY WOULDN'T HAVE HAD ANY SPARE COINS ON YOU, LIKE I DID.

SPEAKING OF WHICH... GOT ANY MORE MONEY ON YOU, SCROOGE?

YUP! PRETTY SIMPLE WHEN YOU THINK ABOUT IT.

JUST LIKE THE THREE OF YOU! SIMPLE! NOW GET LOST!

WHAT DO YOU MEAN? WHERE WOULD WE GO?

HMMM...

WHAT'S THE PLAN NOW?

I DON'T KNOW WHAT YOU GENIUSES HAVE IN MIND, BUT I'M GOING BACK TO THE BIN!

GREAT! WE'LL COME, TOO!

TI-TLIN

MEANWHILE...

HEY CLOVER BOY... NEED A RIDE?

THIS IS THE *PETE-MOBILE*, FILLED WITH MY ENTIRE ARSENAL, COMING YOUR WAY! *HAW, HAW!*

RAT-RAT-RAT

BANG

BANG

HMM...LOOKS LIKE YOU MISSED.

RARR! TAKE THIS! AND THIS! AND THAT! AND THIS!

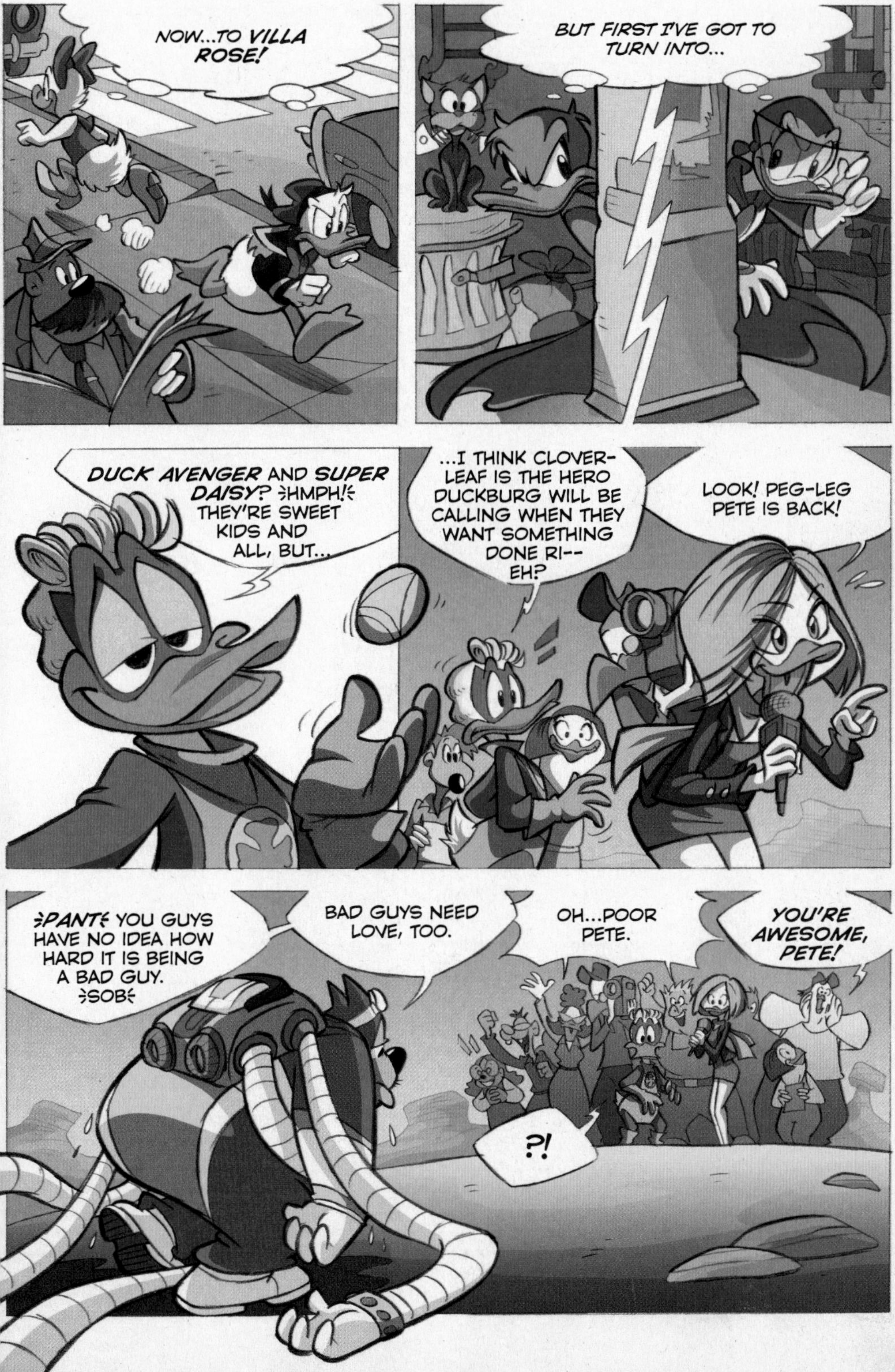
NOW...TO VILLA ROSE!
BUT FIRST I'VE GOT TO TURN INTO...
DUCK AVENGER AND SUPER DAISY? HMPH! THEY'RE SWEET KIDS AND ALL, BUT...
...I THINK CLOVER-LEAF IS THE HERO DUCKBURG WILL BE CALLING WHEN THEY WANT SOMETHING DONE RI-- EH?
LOOK! PEG-LEG PETE IS BACK!
PANT YOU GUYS HAVE NO IDEA HOW HARD IT IS BEING A BAD GUY. SOB
BAD GUYS NEED LOVE, TOO.
OH...POOR PETE.
YOU'RE AWESOME, PETE!
?!

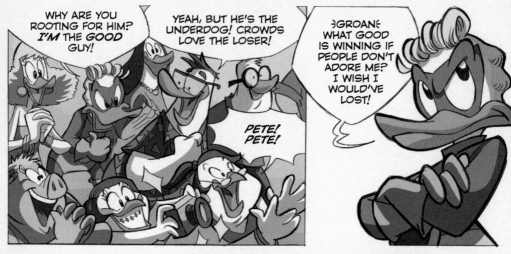

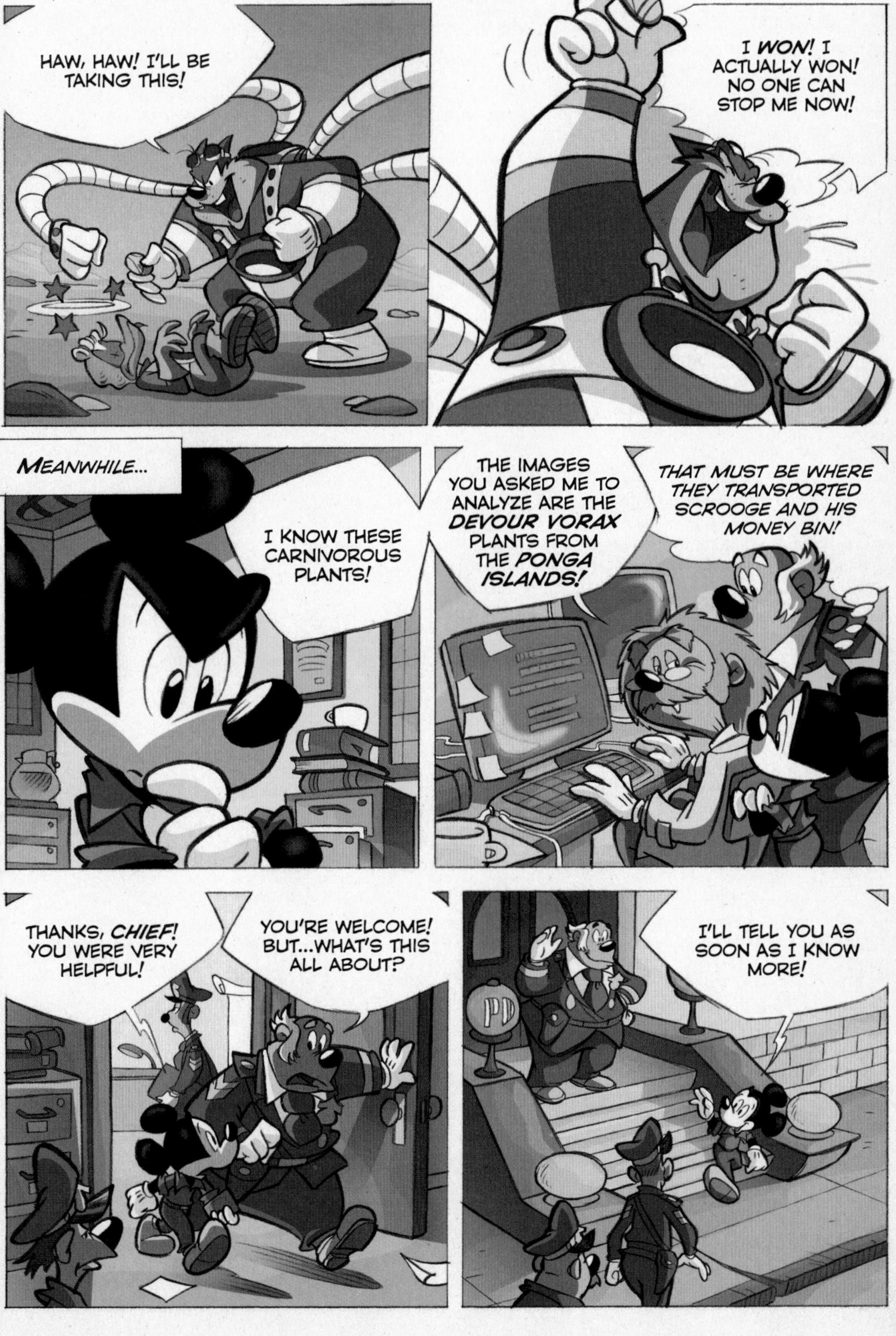
HAW, HAW! I'LL BE TAKING THIS!
I WON! I ACTUALLY WON! NO ONE CAN STOP ME NOW!
MEANWHILE...
I KNOW THESE CARNIVOROUS PLANTS!
THE IMAGES YOU ASKED ME TO ANALYZE ARE THE DEVOUR VORAX PLANTS FROM THE PONGA ISLANDS!
THAT MUST BE WHERE THEY TRANSPORTED SCROOGE AND HIS MONEY BIN!
THANKS, CHIEF! YOU WERE VERY HELPFUL!
YOU'RE WELCOME! BUT...WHAT'S THIS ALL ABOUT?
I'LL TELL YOU AS SOON AS I KNOW MORE!

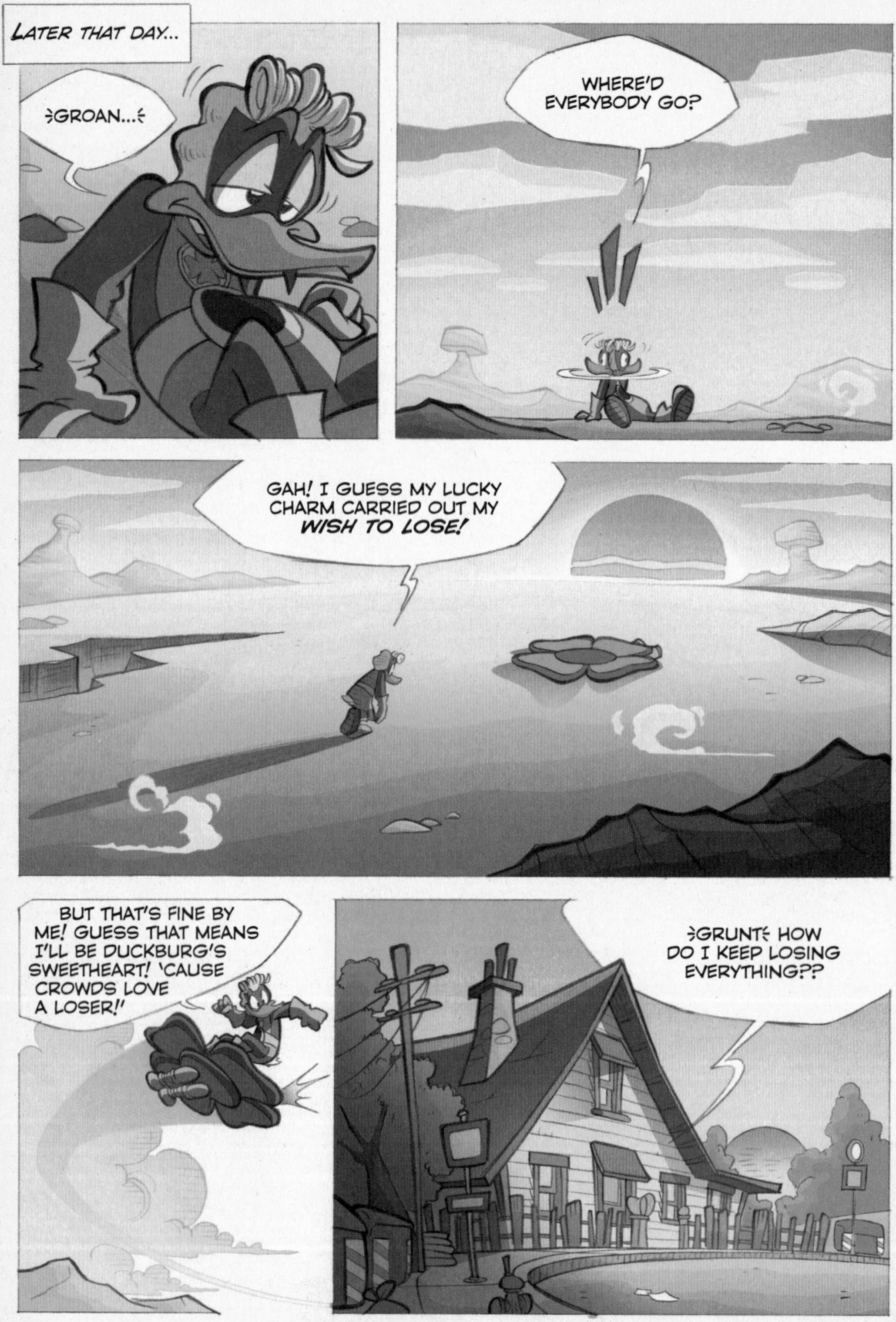
LATER THAT DAY...
⁓GROAN...⁓
WHERE'D EVERYBODY GO?
GAH! I GUESS MY LUCKY CHARM CARRIED OUT MY WISH TO LOSE!
BUT THAT'S FINE BY ME! GUESS THAT MEANS I'LL BE DUCKBURG'S SWEETHEART! 'CAUSE CROWDS LOVE A LOSER!
⁓GRUNT⁓ HOW DO I KEEP LOSING EVERYTHING??

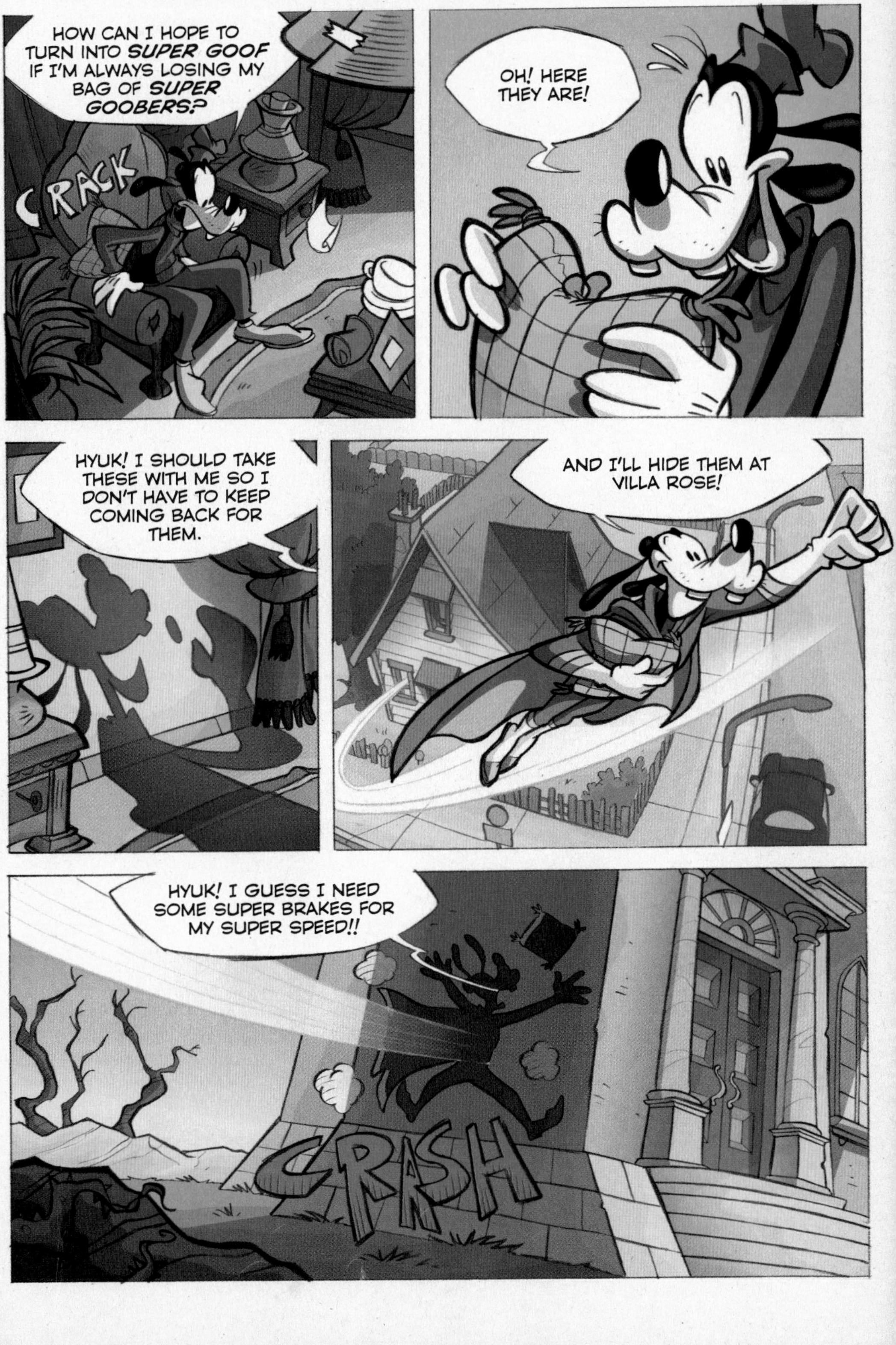
HOW CAN I HOPE TO TURN INTO SUPER GOOF IF I'M ALWAYS LOSING MY BAG OF SUPER GOOBERS?
CRACK
OH! HERE THEY ARE!
HYUK! I SHOULD TAKE THESE WITH ME SO I DON'T HAVE TO KEEP COMING BACK FOR THEM.
AND I'LL HIDE THEM AT VILLA ROSE!
HYUK! I GUESS I NEED SOME SUPER BRAKES FOR MY SUPER SPEED!!
CRASH

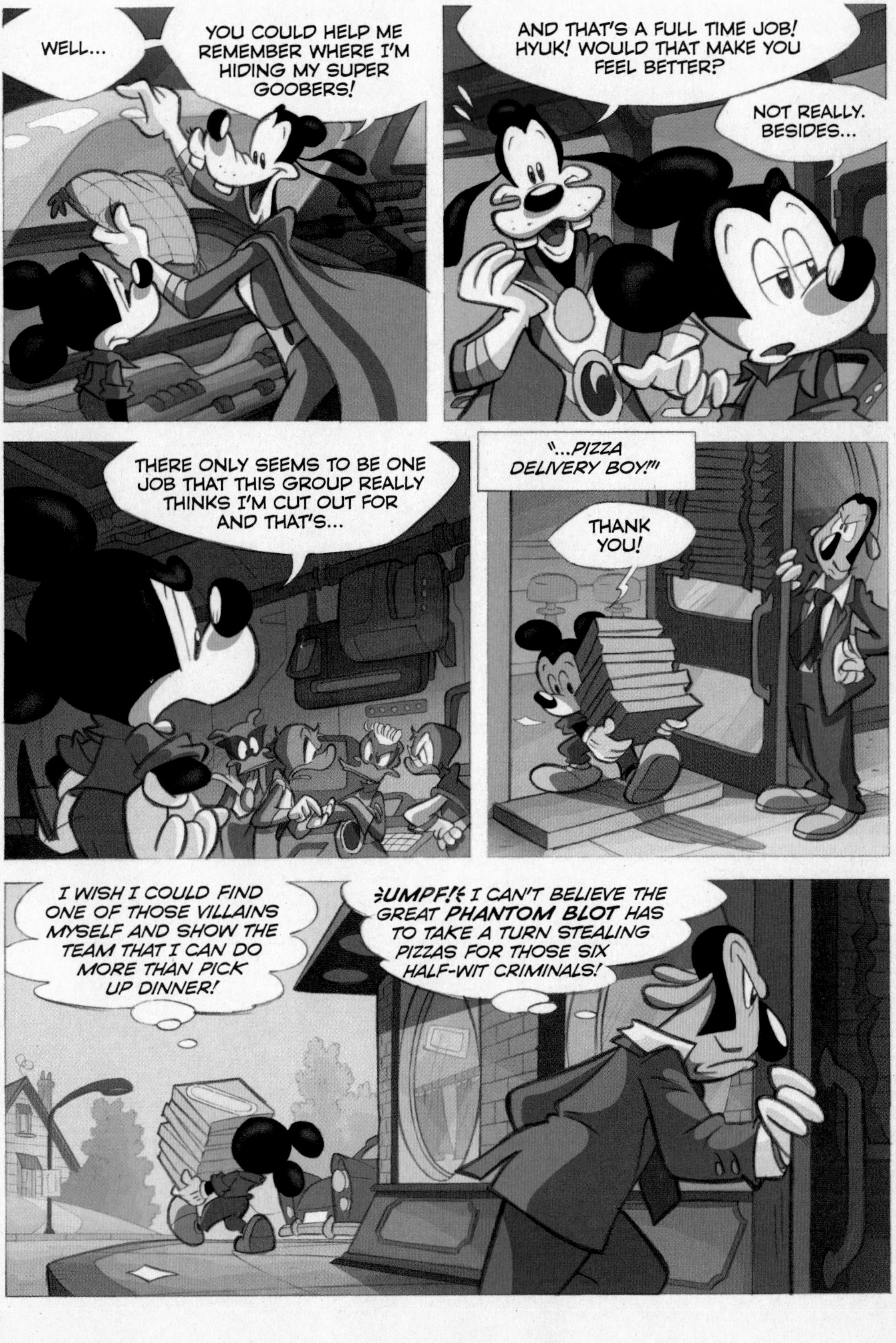
WELL...
YOU COULD HELP ME REMEMBER WHERE I'M HIDING MY SUPER GOOBERS!
AND THAT'S A FULL TIME JOB! HYUK! WOULD THAT MAKE YOU FEEL BETTER?
NOT REALLY. BESIDES...
THERE ONLY SEEMS TO BE ONE JOB THAT THIS GROUP REALLY THINKS I'M CUT OUT FOR AND THAT'S...
"...PIZZA DELIVERY BOY!"
THANK YOU!
I WISH I COULD FIND ONE OF THOSE VILLAINS MYSELF AND SHOW THE TEAM THAT I CAN DO MORE THAN PICK UP DINNER!
HUMPF! I CAN'T BELIEVE THE GREAT PHANTOM BLOT HAS TO TAKE A TURN STEALING PIZZAS FOR THOSE SIX HALF-WIT CRIMINALS!

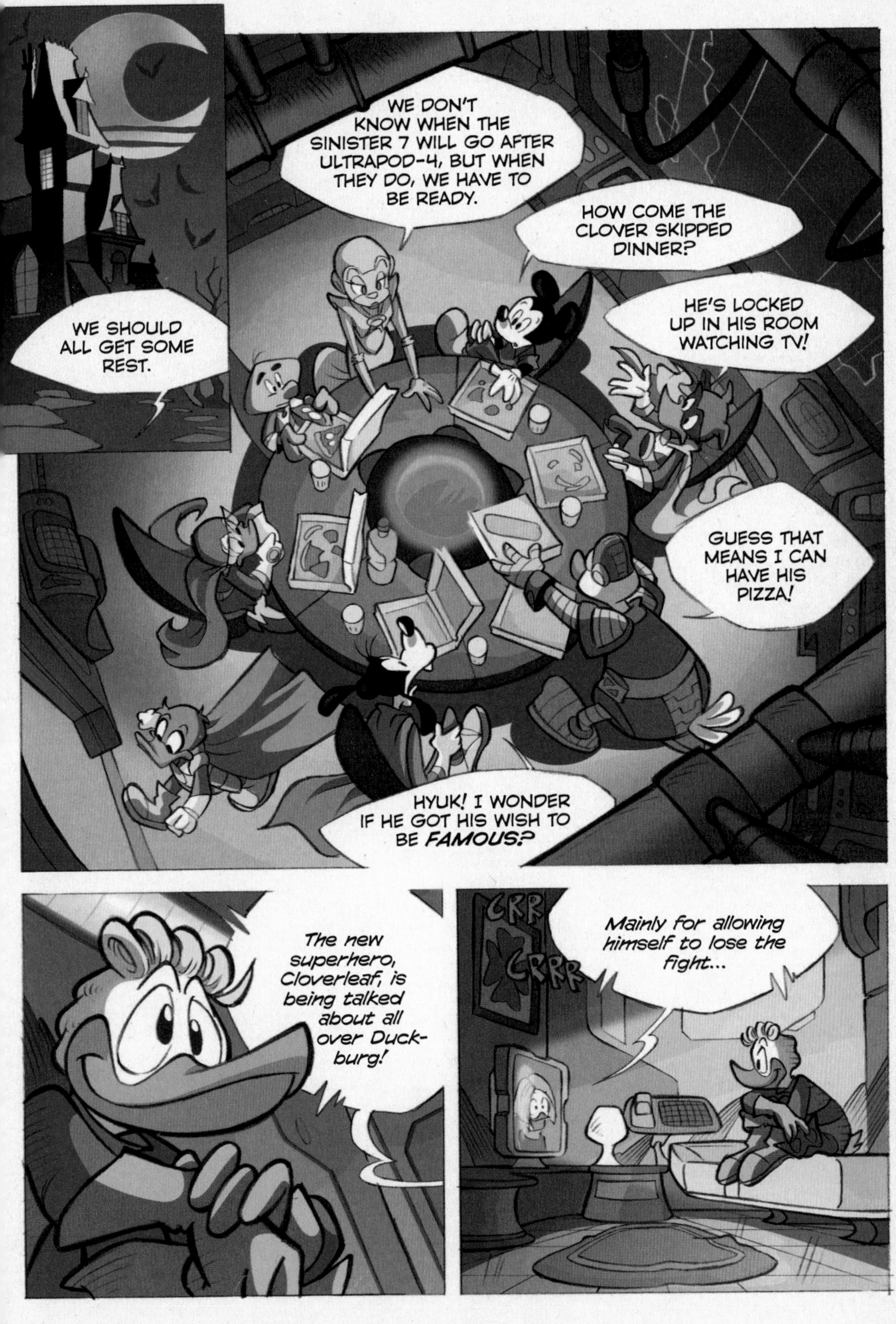
WE SHOULD ALL GET SOME REST.
WE DON'T KNOW WHEN THE SINISTER 7 WILL GO AFTER ULTRAPOD-4, BUT WHEN THEY DO, WE HAVE TO BE READY.
HOW COME THE CLOVER SKIPPED DINNER?
HE'S LOCKED UP IN HIS ROOM WATCHING TV!
GUESS THAT MEANS I CAN HAVE HIS PIZZA!
HYUK! I WONDER IF HE GOT HIS WISH TO BE FAMOUS?
The new superhero, Cloverleaf, is being talked about all over Duck-burg!
CRR CRRR
Mainly for allowing himself to lose the fight...

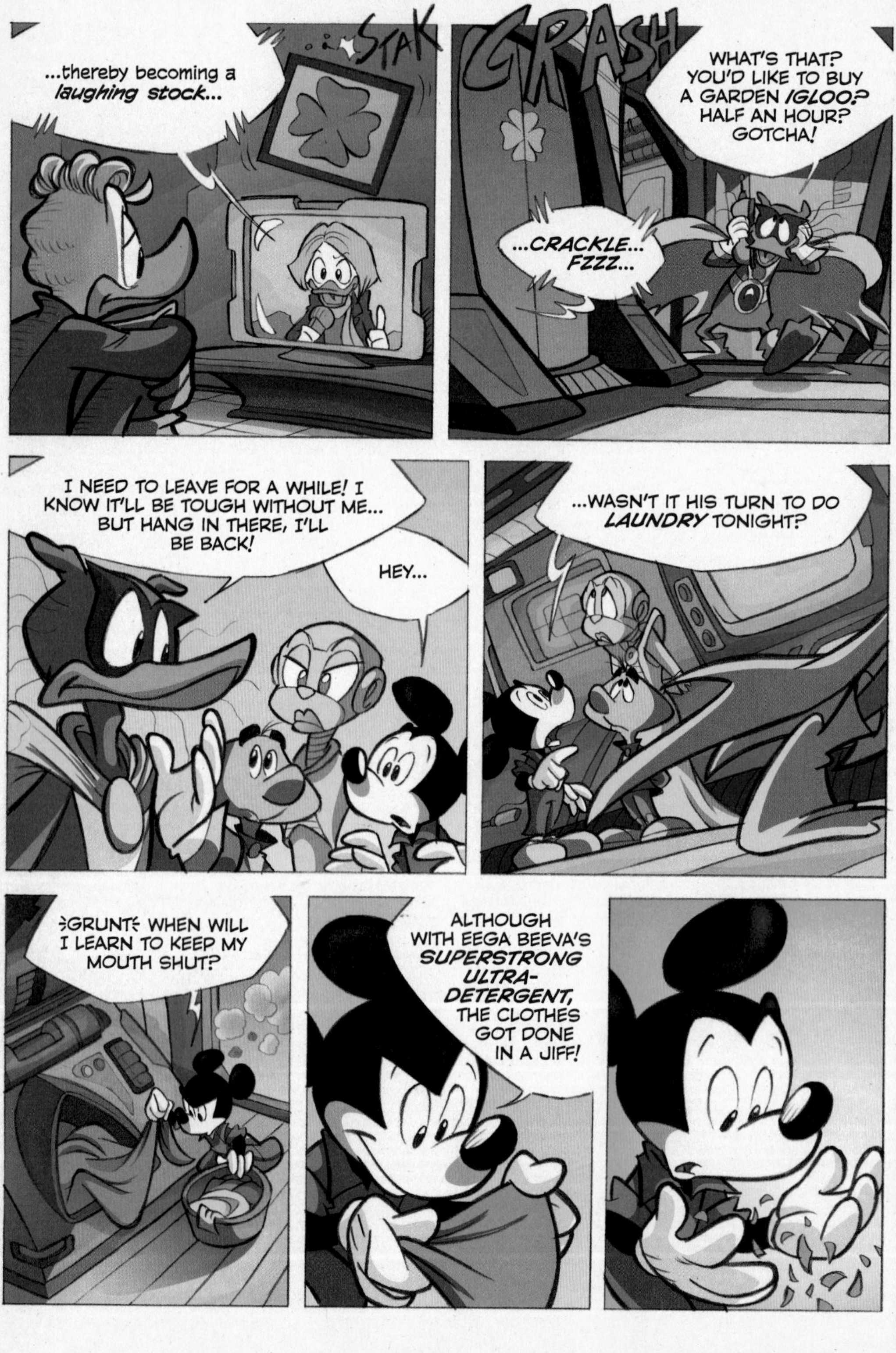
...thereby becoming a *laughing stock*...
STAK
CRASH
WHAT'S THAT? YOU'D LIKE TO BUY A GARDEN *IGLOO?* HALF AN HOUR? GOTCHA!
...CRACKLE... FZZZ...
I NEED TO LEAVE FOR A WHILE! I KNOW IT'LL BE TOUGH WITHOUT ME... BUT HANG IN THERE, I'LL BE BACK!
HEY...
...WASN'T IT HIS TURN TO DO *LAUNDRY* TONIGHT?
GRUNT WHEN WILL I LEARN TO KEEP MY MOUTH SHUT?
ALTHOUGH WITH EEGA BEEVA'S *SUPERSTRONG ULTRA-DETERGENT,* THE CLOTHES GOT DONE IN A JIFF!

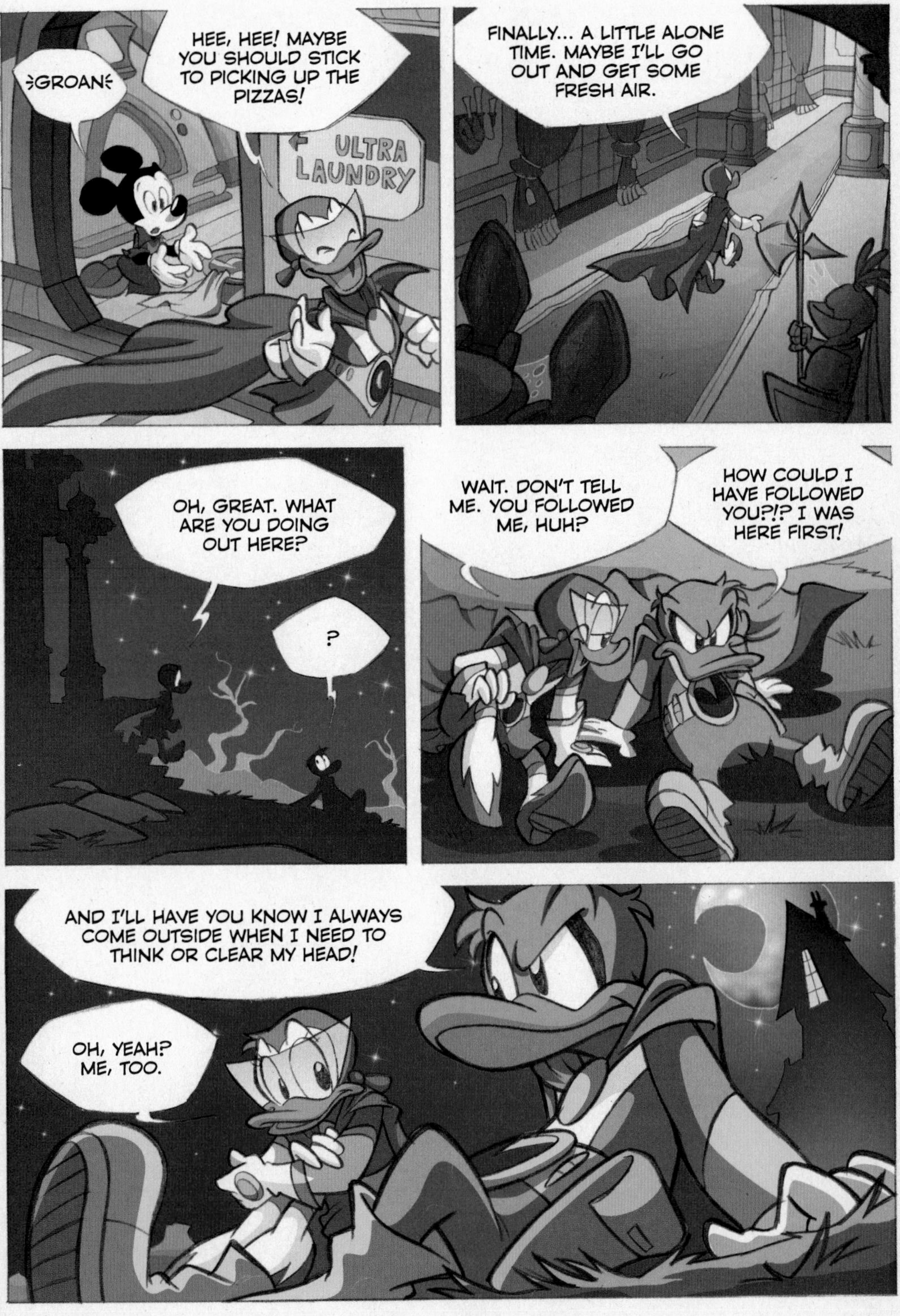
HEE, HEE! MAYBE YOU SHOULD STICK TO PICKING UP THE PIZZAS!
GROAN
ULTRA LAUNDRY
FINALLY... A LITTLE ALONE TIME. MAYBE I'LL GO OUT AND GET SOME FRESH AIR.
OH, GREAT. WHAT ARE YOU DOING OUT HERE?
?
WAIT. DON'T TELL ME. YOU FOLLOWED ME, HUH?
HOW COULD I HAVE FOLLOWED YOU?!? I WAS HERE FIRST!
AND I'LL HAVE YOU KNOW I ALWAYS COME OUTSIDE WHEN I NEED TO THINK OR CLEAR MY HEAD!
OH, YEAH? ME, TOO.

AROUND BEDTIME...

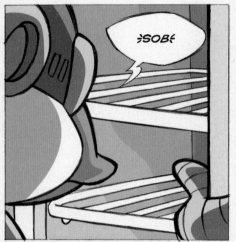

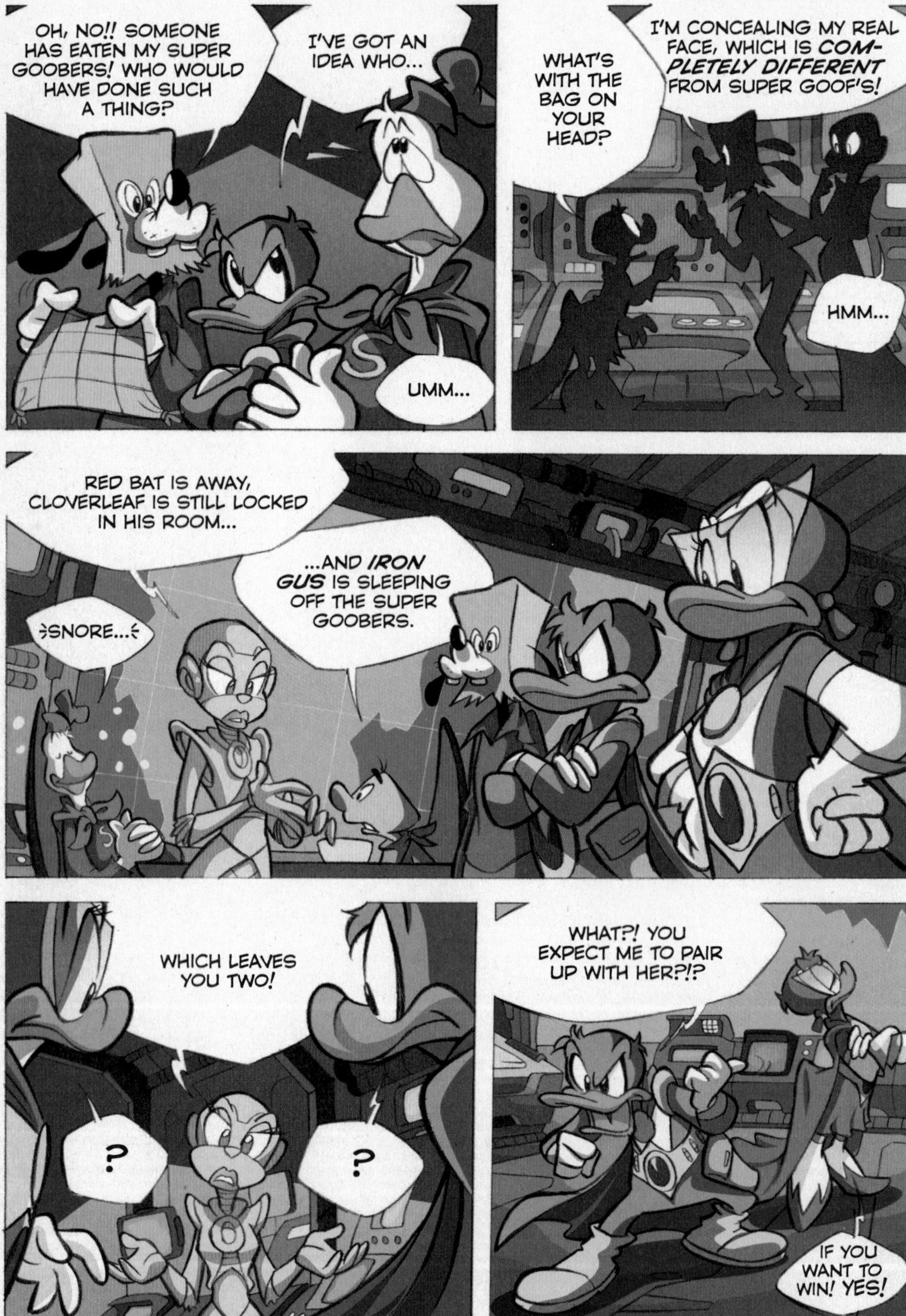

OH, NO!! SOMEONE HAS EATEN MY SUPER GOOBERS! WHO WOULD HAVE DONE SUCH A THING?
I'VE GOT AN IDEA WHO...
UMM...
WHAT'S WITH THE BAG ON YOUR HEAD?
I'M CONCEALING MY REAL FACE, WHICH IS *COMPLETELY DIFFERENT* FROM SUPER GOOF'S!
HMM...
RED BAT IS AWAY, CLOVERLEAF IS STILL LOCKED IN HIS ROOM...
...AND *IRON GUS* IS SLEEPING OFF THE SUPER GOOBERS.
SNORE...
WHICH LEAVES YOU TWO!
?
?
WHAT?! YOU EXPECT ME TO PAIR UP WITH HER?!?
IF YOU WANT TO WIN! YES!

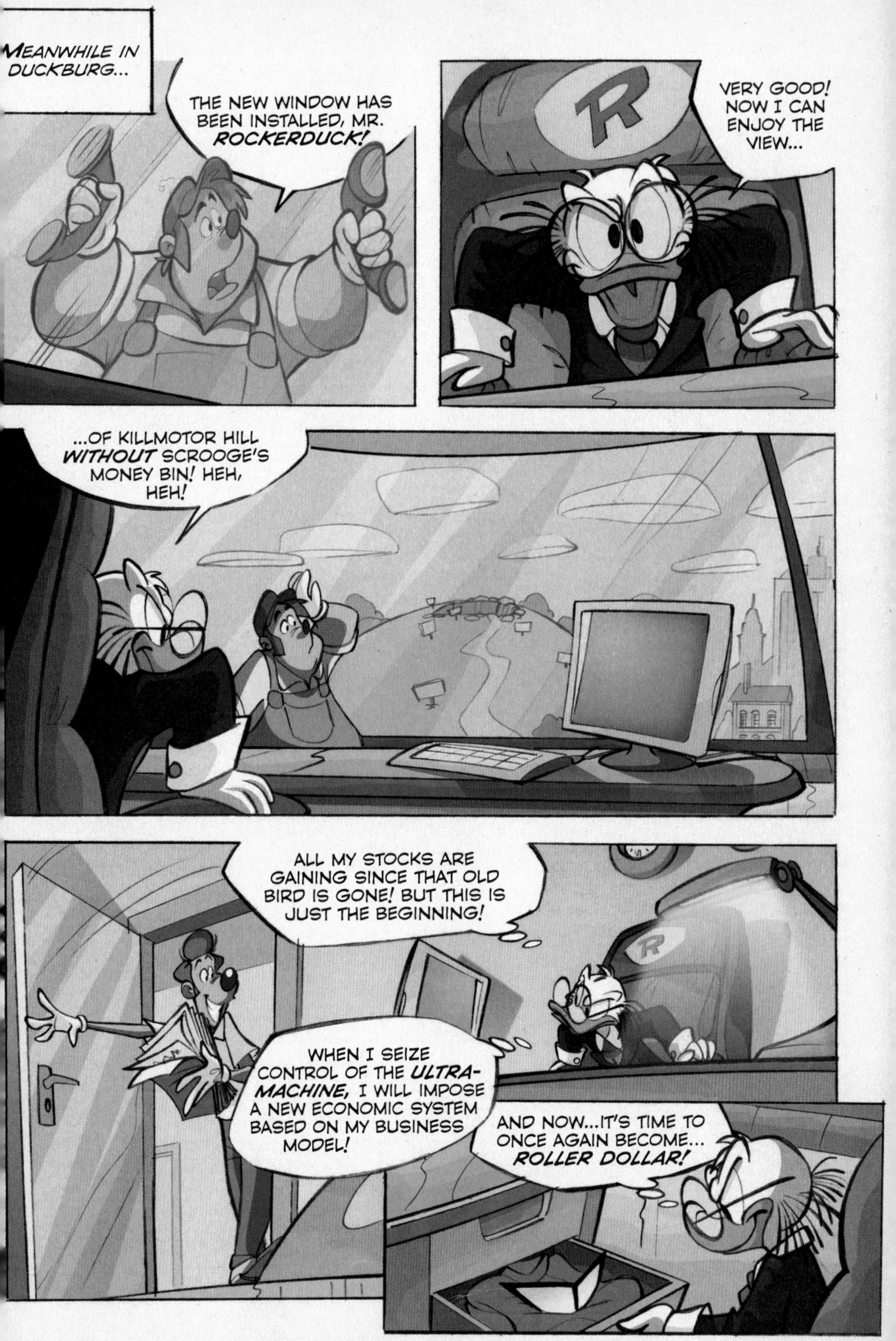
MEANWHILE IN DUCKBURG...
THE NEW WINDOW HAS BEEN INSTALLED, MR. ROCKERDUCK!
VERY GOOD! NOW I CAN ENJOY THE VIEW...
...OF KILLMOTOR HILL WITHOUT SCROOGE'S MONEY BIN! HEH, HEH!
ALL MY STOCKS ARE GAINING SINCE THAT OLD BIRD IS GONE! BUT THIS IS JUST THE BEGINNING!
WHEN I SEIZE CONTROL OF THE ULTRA-MACHINE, I WILL IMPOSE A NEW ECONOMIC SYSTEM BASED ON MY BUSINESS MODEL!
AND NOW...IT'S TIME TO ONCE AGAIN BECOME... ROLLER DOLLAR!

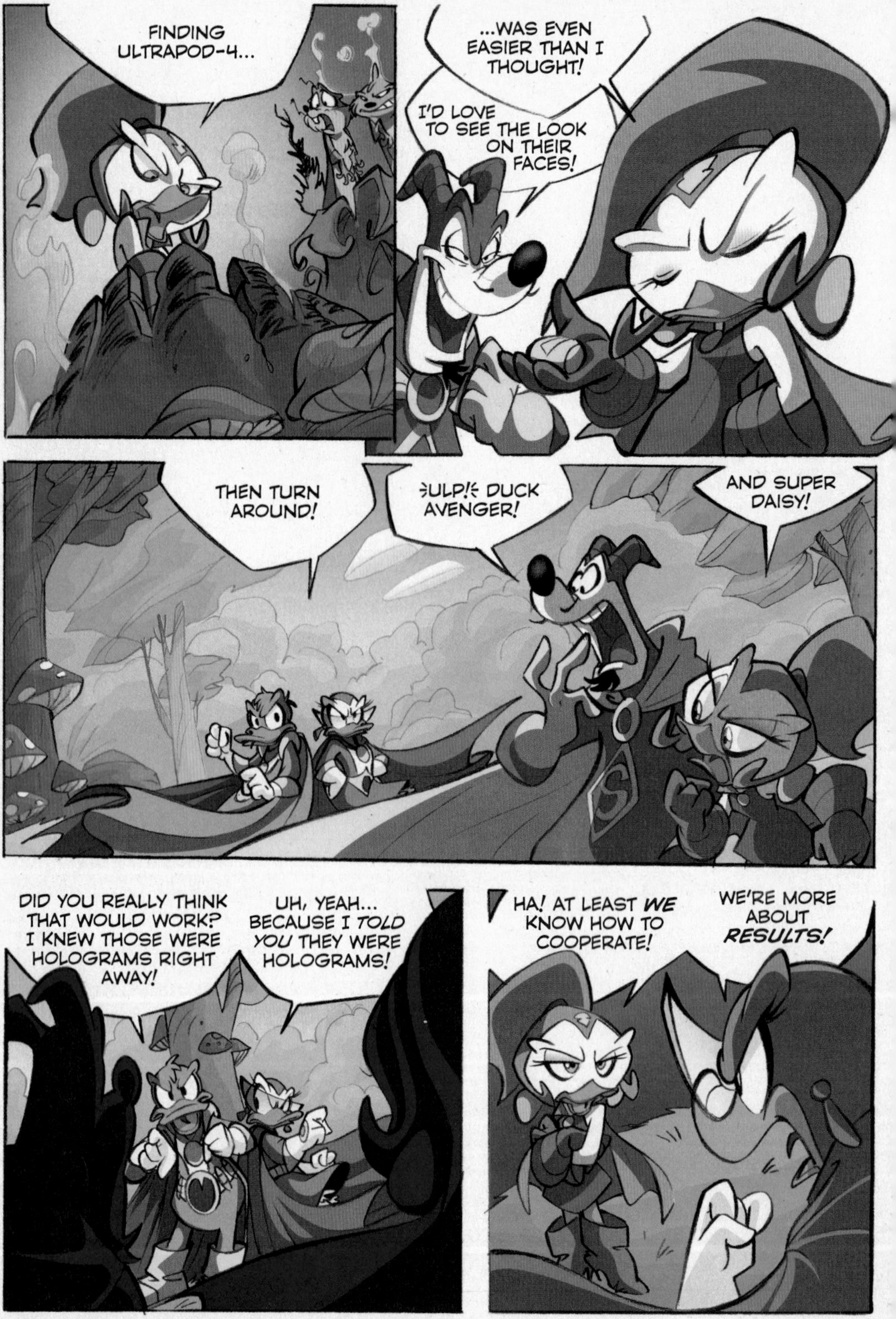
FINDING ULTRAPOD-4...
...WAS EVEN EASIER THAN I THOUGHT!
I'D LOVE TO SEE THE LOOK ON THEIR FACES!
THEN TURN AROUND!
GULP! DUCK AVENGER!
AND SUPER DAISY!
DID YOU REALLY THINK THAT WOULD WORK? I KNEW THOSE WERE HOLOGRAMS RIGHT AWAY!
UH, YEAH... BECAUSE I *TOLD YOU* THEY WERE HOLOGRAMS!
HA! AT LEAST ***WE*** KNOW HOW TO COOPERATE!
WE'RE MORE ABOUT ***RESULTS!***

GOOD LUCK HITTING ME WHEN YOU CAN'T SEE ME!

TURNING *INVISIBLE* WON'T HELP YOU!

BUT IT WILL HURT YOU!

EEEK!

SWISH

HEY, MY *GLOVES!*

TAKE THIS!

OOOF!

YESSS! THROWING MY VOICE REALLY HELPED TO CONFUSE HER!

OH, NO! THIS IS THE FAKE ULTRAPOD!

BUT MY POWERS ARE REAL! THE GLOVES ARE ONLY A *SLIGHT* ENHANCEMENT!

MEANWHILE, IN HIS ROOM AT VILLA ROSE...

NOW TO READ THE GOOSE-A-RAMA FORUMS.

I'M SURE MY FANS ARE SPEAKING OUT!

PegLeg Pete — 200 comments:
He's the most likable! 😊 Sbrodol
Pete U are legendary! 😊 Sgrinfla

Super Goof — 120 comments:
Still the most super! 😊 Gilberto
I like him a lot! 😊 XSmurf

UM...

DON'T CARE ABOUT THESE... I WANNA SEE COMMENTS ABOUT ME!

Inquinator — 1 comment:
He's my hero, I don't like to take baths either! 😊 Babybot

Cloverleaf — 1827 comments:
Who needs him? He's so unlikable! ☹ Pik36
I can't stand him! ☹ BillyG

WHAAAT?! FOR THE FIRST TIME PEOPLE ARE TALKING ABOUT ME...

CLIC

...AND I DON'T LIKE IT!

WAIT! I'VE GOT AN IDEA!

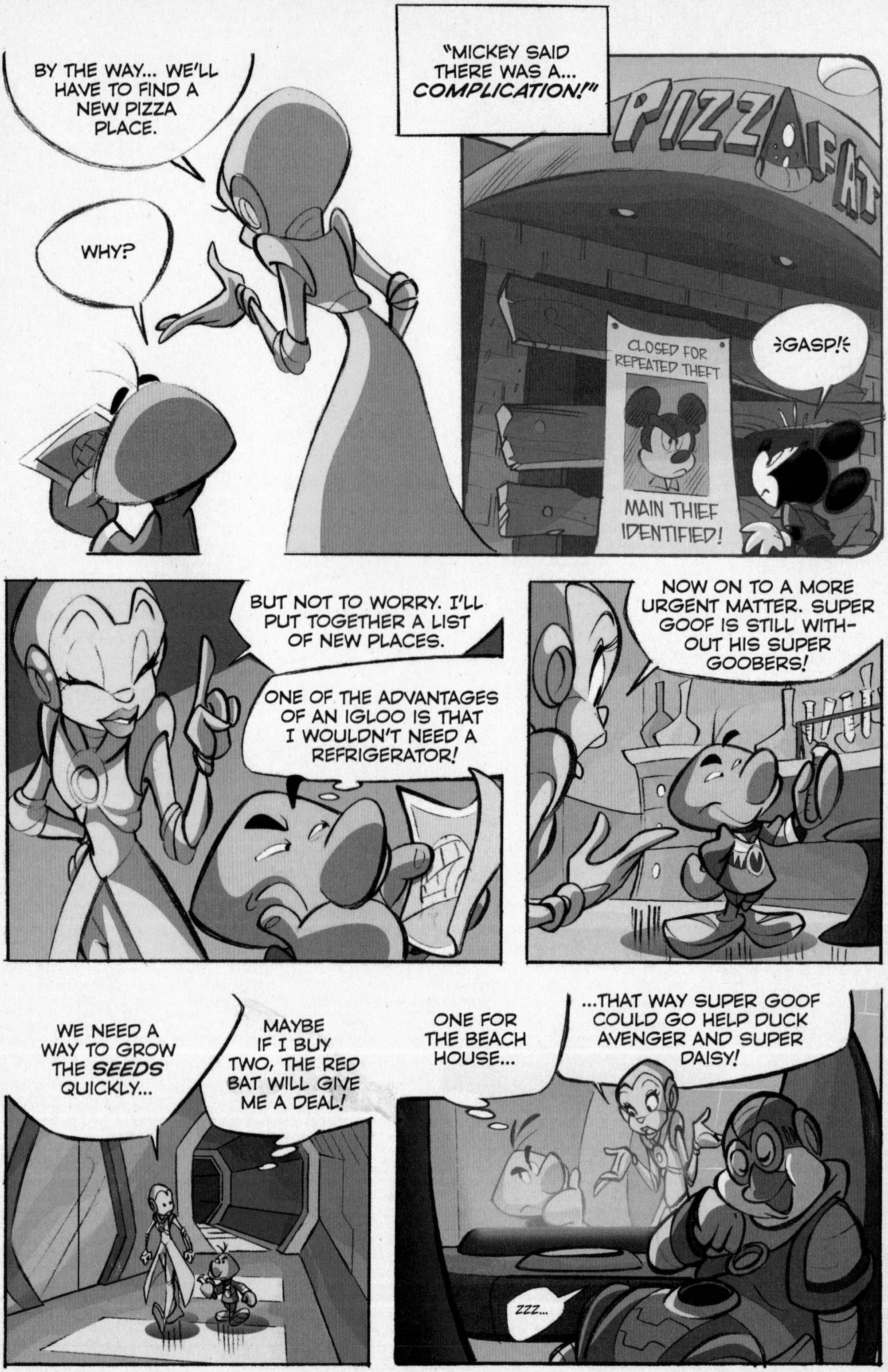
BY THE WAY... WE'LL HAVE TO FIND A NEW PIZZA PLACE.
WHY?
"MICKEY SAID THERE WAS A... *COMPLICATION!*"
PIZZA
CLOSED FOR REPEATED THEFT
MAIN THIEF IDENTIFIED!
GASP!
BUT NOT TO WORRY. I'LL PUT TOGETHER A LIST OF NEW PLACES.
ONE OF THE ADVANTAGES OF AN IGLOO IS THAT I WOULDN'T NEED A REFRIGERATOR!
NOW ON TO A MORE URGENT MATTER. SUPER GOOF IS STILL WITH-OUT HIS SUPER GOOBERS!
WE NEED A WAY TO GROW THE *SEEDS* QUICKLY...
MAYBE IF I BUY TWO, THE RED BAT WILL GIVE ME A DEAL!
ONE FOR THE BEACH HOUSE...
...THAT WAY SUPER GOOF COULD GO HELP DUCK AVENGER AND SUPER DAISY!
ZZZ...

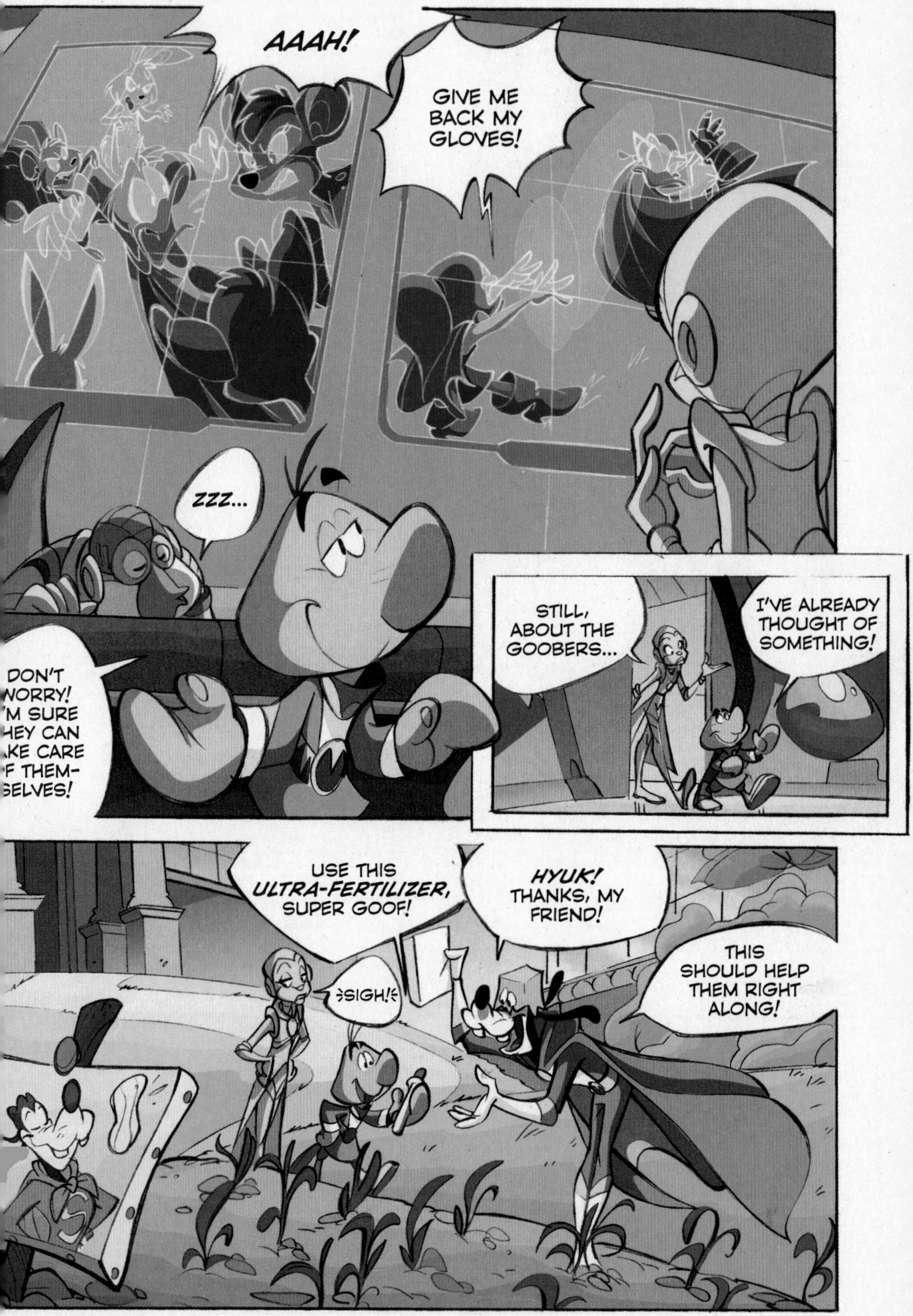
AAAH!
GIVE ME BACK MY GLOVES!
ZZZ...
DON'T WORRY! 'M SURE HEY CAN KE CARE F THEM- SELVES!
STILL, ABOUT THE GOOBERS...
I'VE ALREADY THOUGHT OF SOMETHING!
USE THIS ULTRA-FERTILIZER, SUPER GOOF!
SIGH!
HYUK! THANKS, MY FRIEND!
THIS SHOULD HELP THEM RIGHT ALONG!

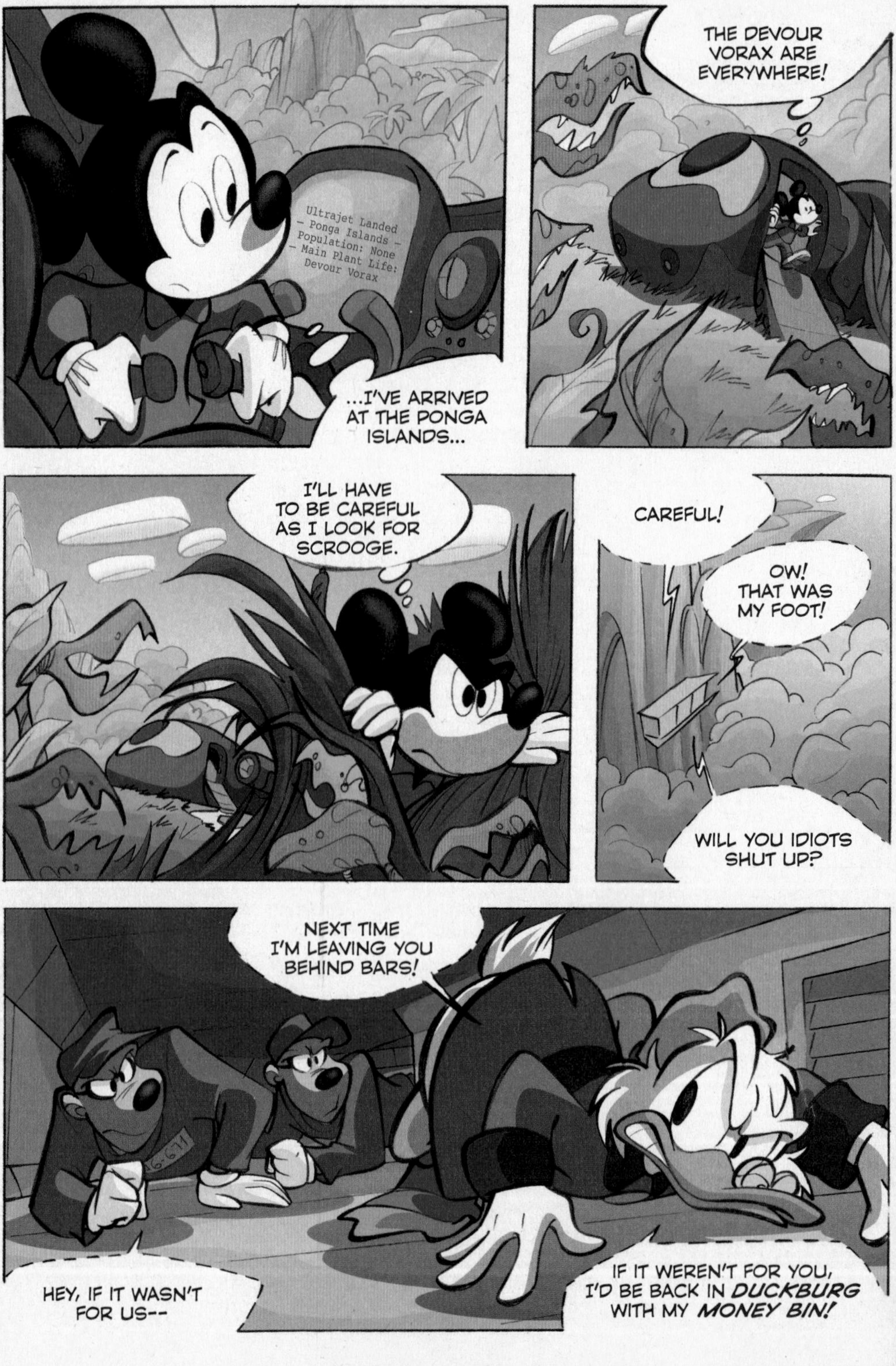
Ultrajet Landed
– Ponga Islands –
Population: None
– Main Plant Life:
Devour Vorax
...I'VE ARRIVED AT THE PONGA ISLANDS...
THE DEVOUR VORAX ARE EVERYWHERE!
I'LL HAVE TO BE CAREFUL AS I LOOK FOR SCROOGE.
CAREFUL!
OW! THAT WAS MY FOOT!
WILL YOU IDIOTS SHUT UP?
NEXT TIME I'M LEAVING YOU BEHIND BARS!
HEY, IF IT WASN'T FOR US--
IF IT WEREN'T FOR YOU, I'D BE BACK IN *DUCKBURG* WITH MY *MONEY BIN!*

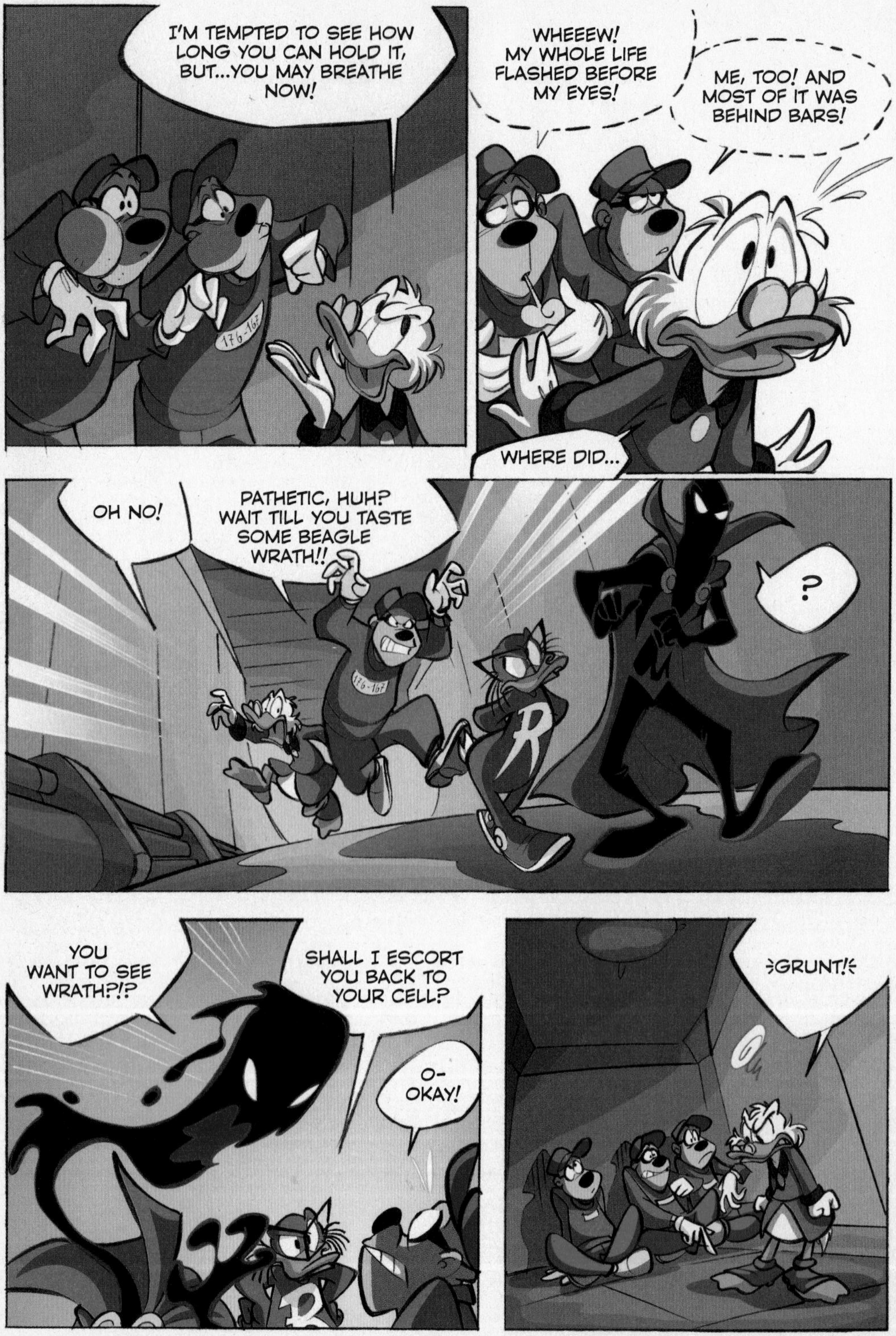
I'M TEMPTED TO SEE HOW LONG YOU CAN HOLD IT, BUT...YOU MAY BREATHE NOW!
WHEEEW! MY WHOLE LIFE FLASHED BEFORE MY EYES!
ME, TOO! AND MOST OF IT WAS BEHIND BARS!
WHERE DID...
OH NO!
PATHETIC, HUH? WAIT TILL YOU TASTE SOME BEAGLE WRATH!!
?
YOU WANT TO SEE WRATH?!?
SHALL I ESCORT YOU BACK TO YOUR CELL?
O-OKAY!
GRUNT!

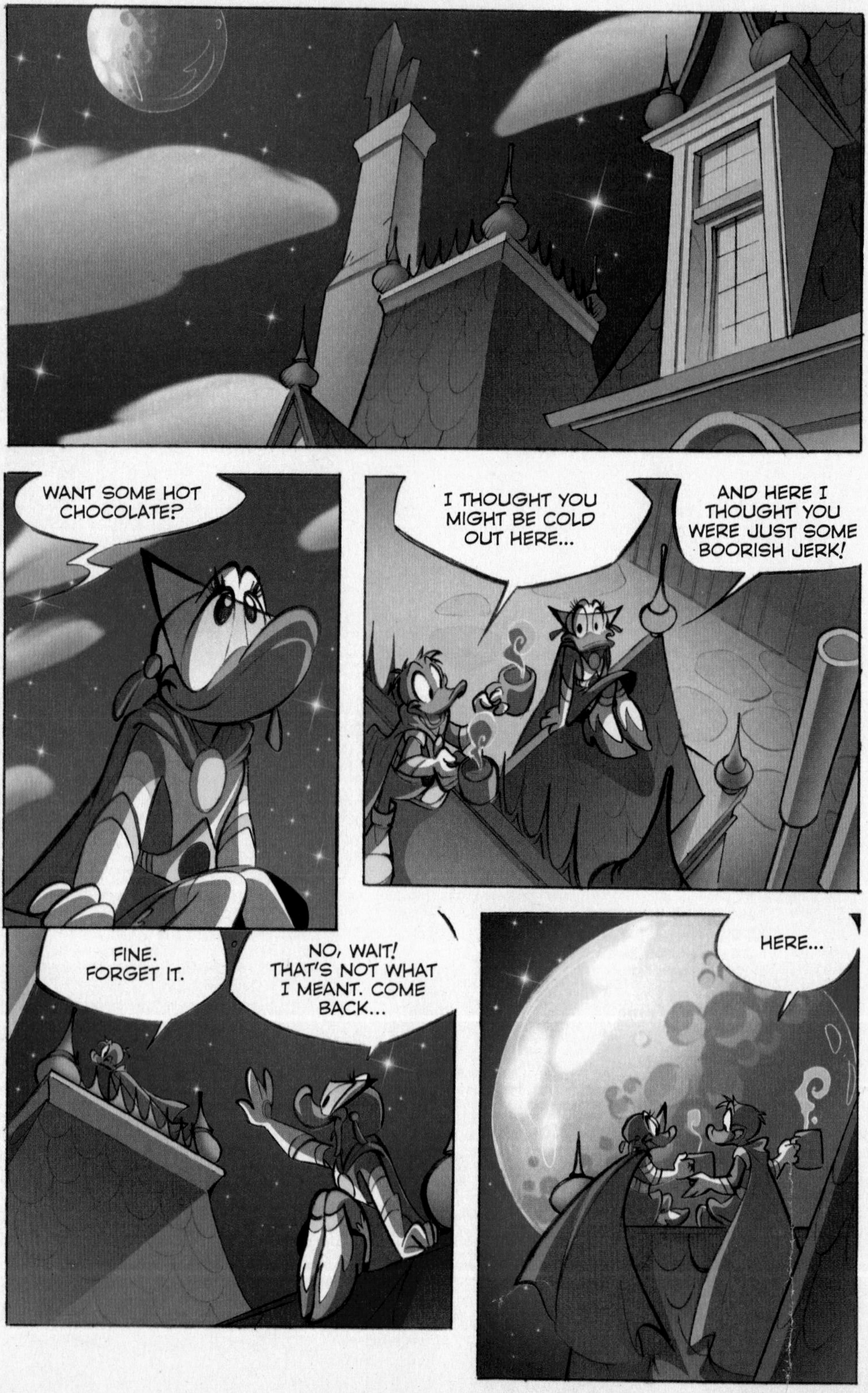
WANT SOME HOT CHOCOLATE?
I THOUGHT YOU MIGHT BE COLD OUT HERE...
AND HERE I THOUGHT YOU WERE JUST SOME BOORISH JERK!
FINE. FORGET IT.
NO, WAIT! THAT'S NOT WHAT I MEANT. COME BACK...
HERE...

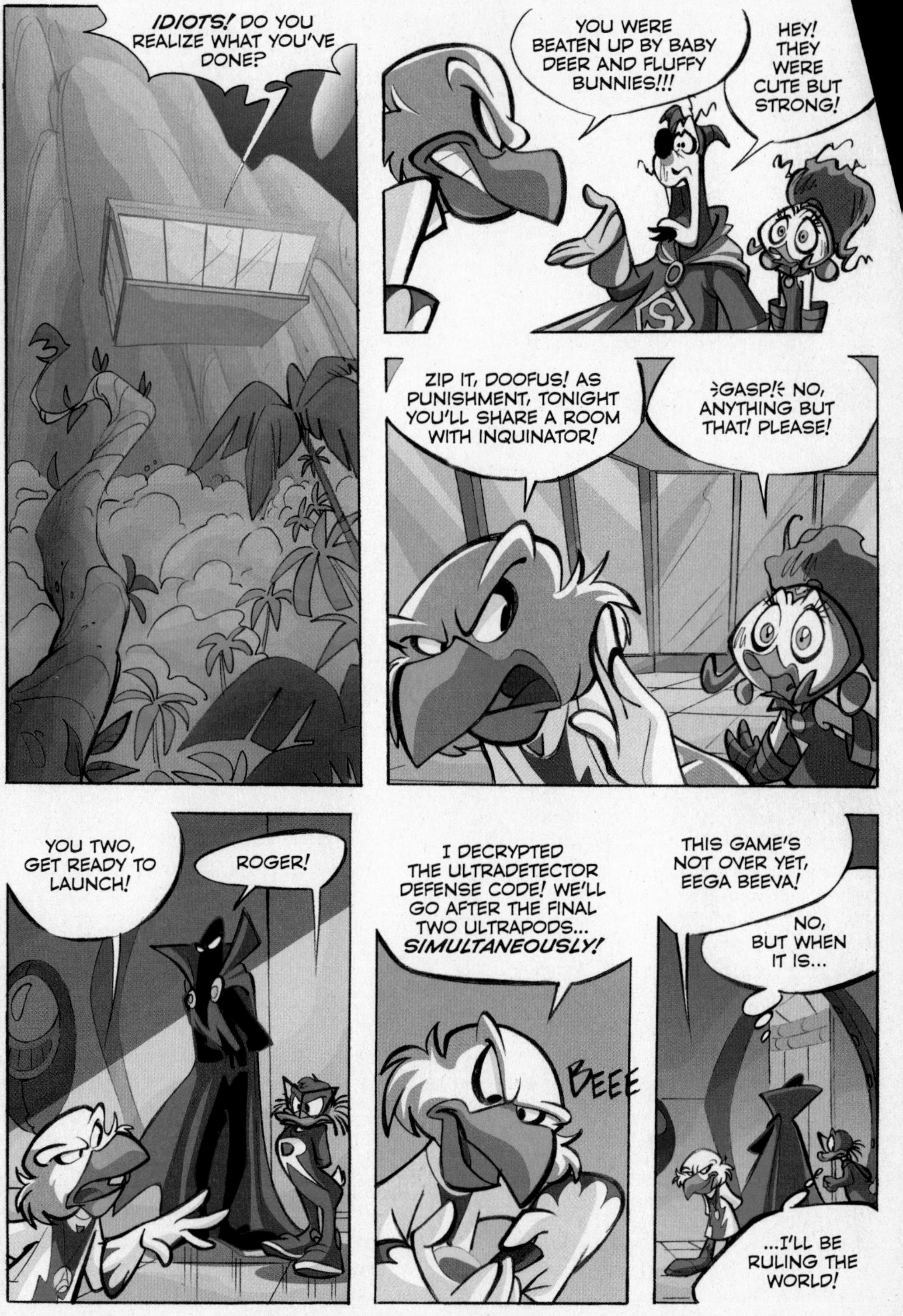
IDIOTS! DO YOU REALIZE WHAT YOU'VE DONE?
YOU WERE BEATEN UP BY BABY DEER AND FLUFFY BUNNIES!!!
HEY! THEY WERE CUTE BUT STRONG!
ZIP IT, DOOFUS! AS PUNISHMENT, TONIGHT YOU'LL SHARE A ROOM WITH INQUINATOR!
GASP! NO, ANYTHING BUT THAT! PLEASE!
YOU TWO, GET READY TO LAUNCH!
ROGER!
I DECRYPTED THE ULTRADETECTOR DEFENSE CODE! WE'LL GO AFTER THE FINAL TWO ULTRAPODS... SIMULTANEOUSLY!
BEEE
THIS GAME'S NOT OVER YET, EEGA BEEVA!
NO, BUT WHEN IT IS...
...I'LL BE RULING THE WORLD!

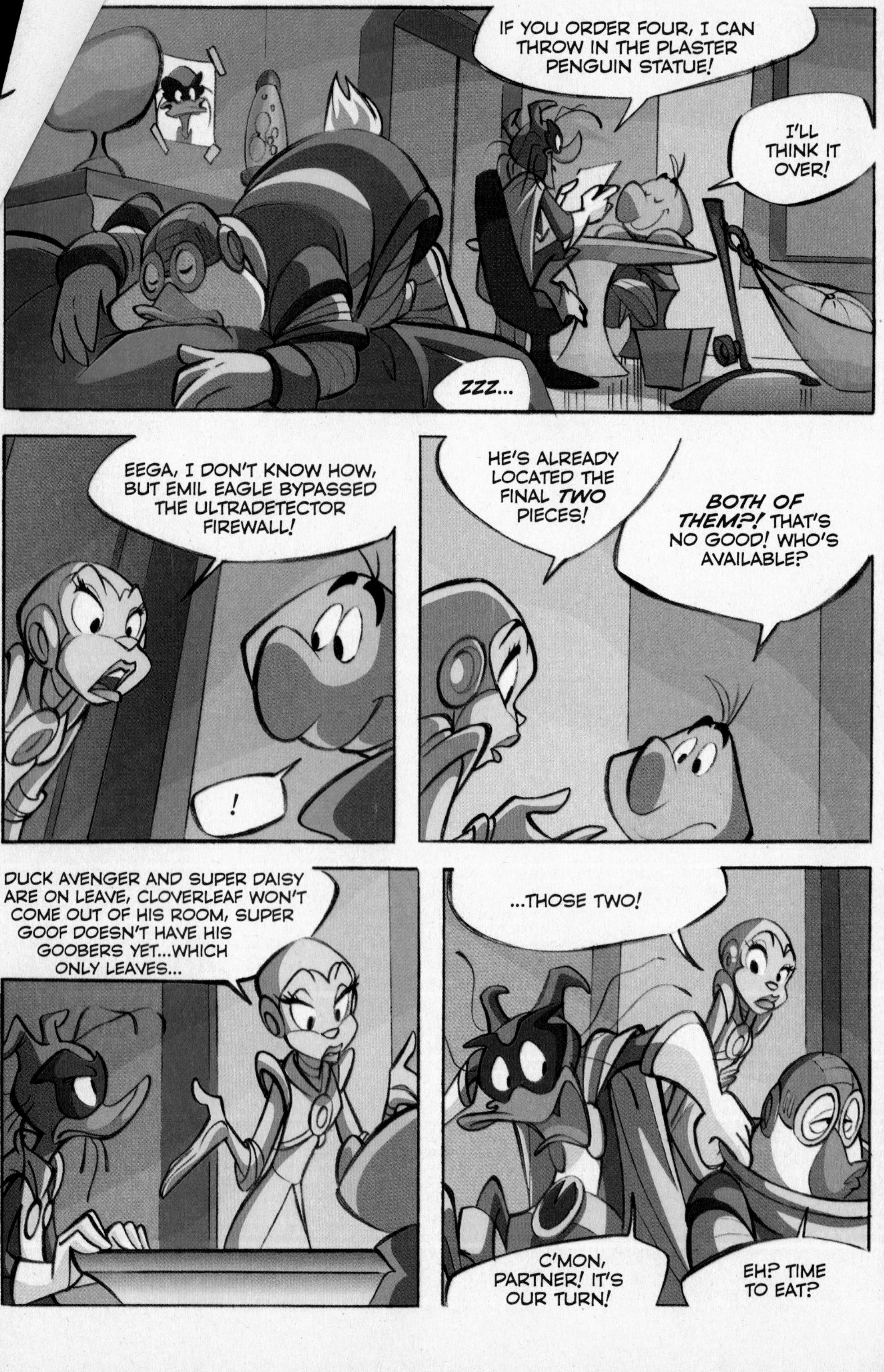
IF YOU ORDER FOUR, I CAN THROW IN THE PLASTER PENGUIN STATUE!
I'LL THINK IT OVER!
ZZZ...
EEGA, I DON'T KNOW HOW, BUT EMIL EAGLE BYPASSED THE ULTRADETECTOR FIREWALL!
!
HE'S ALREADY LOCATED THE FINAL *TWO* PIECES!
BOTH OF THEM?! THAT'S NO GOOD! WHO'S AVAILABLE?
DUCK AVENGER AND SUPER DAISY ARE ON LEAVE, CLOVERLEAF WON'T COME OUT OF HIS ROOM, SUPER GOOF DOESN'T HAVE HIS GOOBERS YET...WHICH ONLY LEAVES...
...THOSE TWO!
C'MON, PARTNER! IT'S OUR TURN!
EH? TIME TO EAT?

DOUBLE WHAMMY! IRON GUS VS. ROLLER DOLLAR AND THE RED BAT VS. THE PHANTOM BLOT! WHO WILL PREVAIL? FIND OUT NEXT TIME!

TO BE CONTINUED...

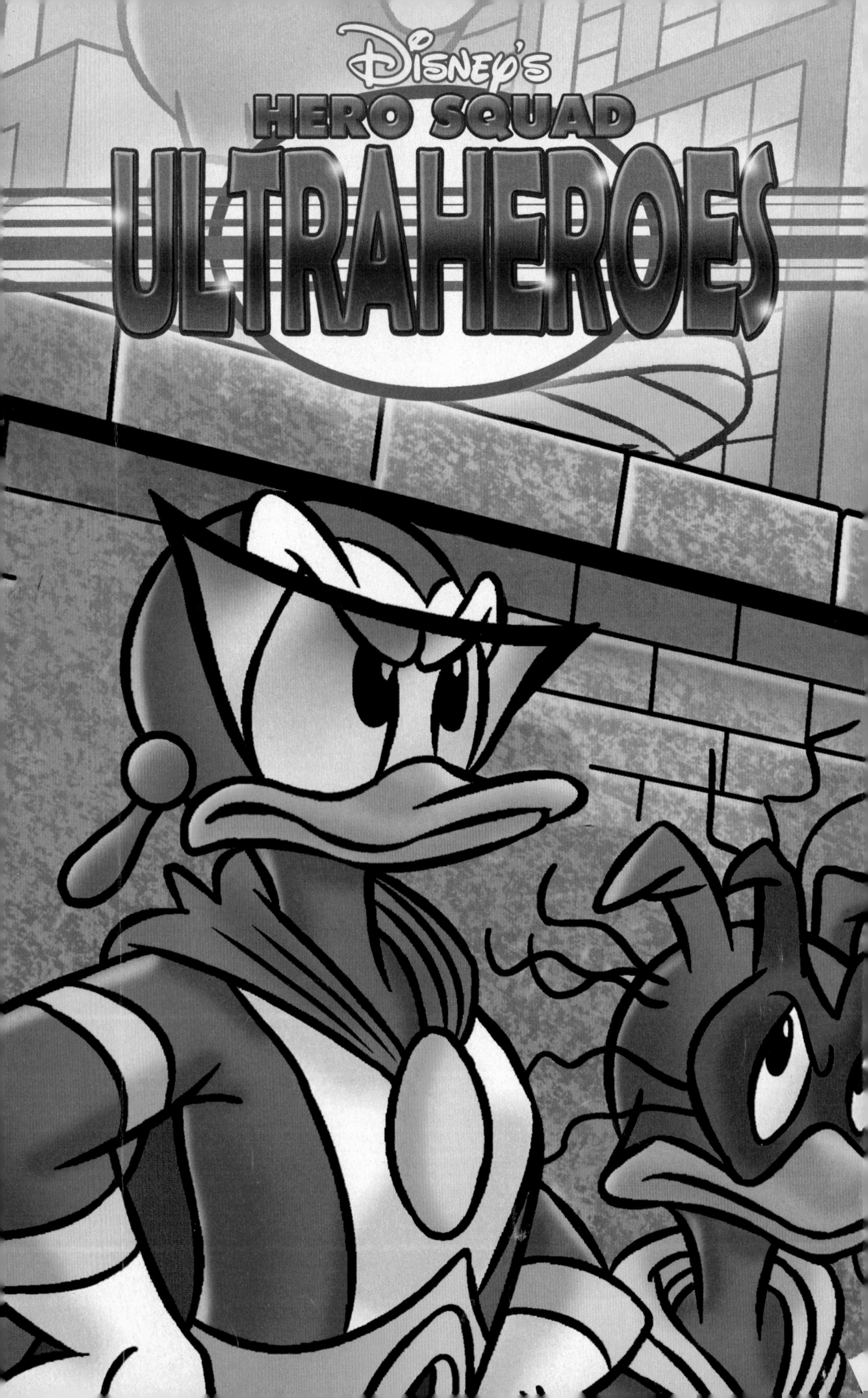
Disney's
HERO SQUAD
ULTRAHEROES

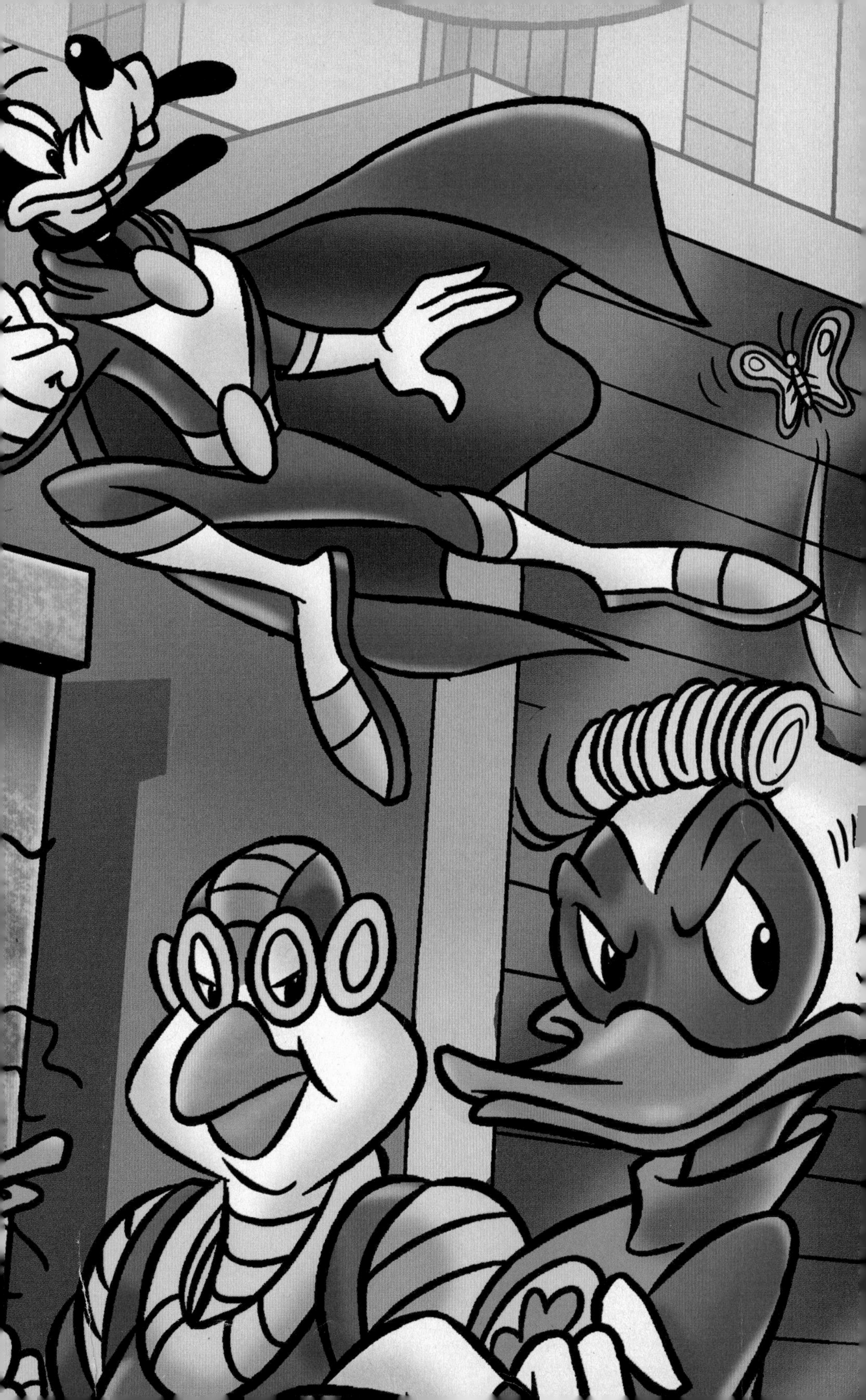

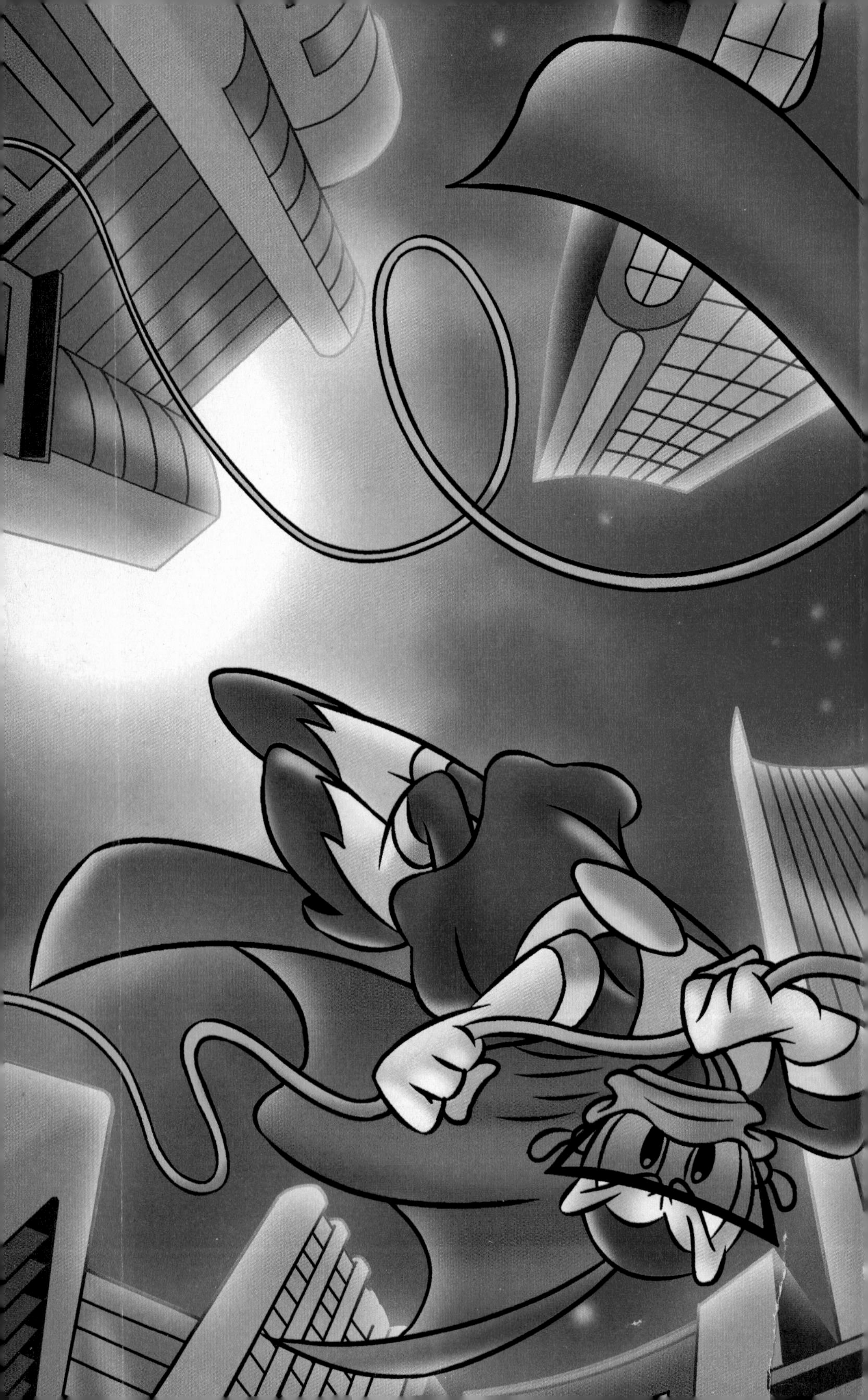

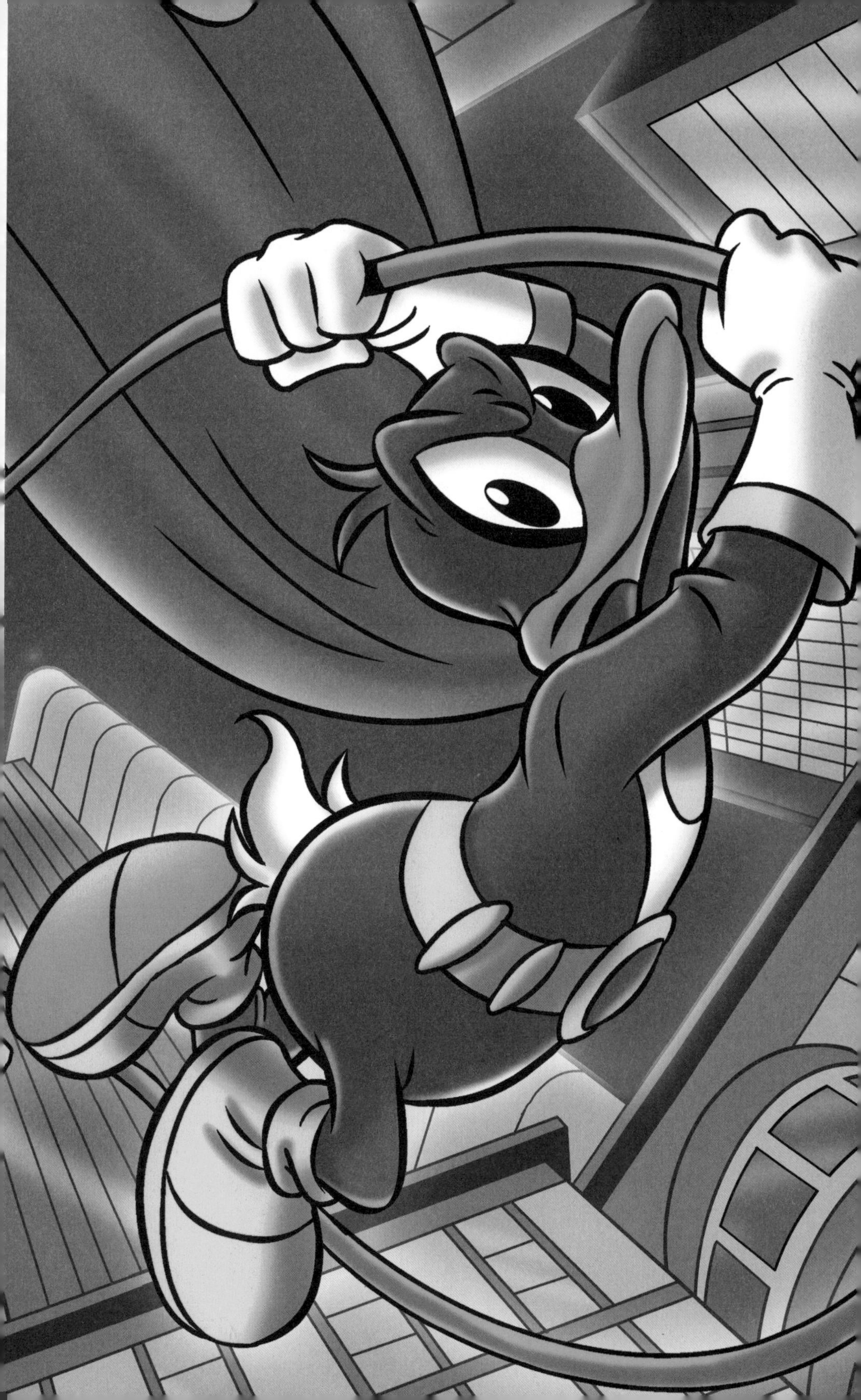